Just a Little Prelude

MERRY FARMER

JUST A LITTLE PRELUDE

Copyright ©2022 by Merry Farmer

This ebook is licensed for your personal enjoyment only. This ebook may not be re-sold or given away to other people. If you would like to share this book with another person, please purchase an additional copy for each recipient. If you're reading this book and did not purchase it, or it was not purchased for your use only, then please return to your digital retailer and purchase your own copy. Thank you for respecting the hard work of this author.

This book is a work of fiction. Names, characters, places, and incidents are products of the author's imagination or are used fictitiously. Any resemblance to actual events or locales or persons, living or dead, is entirely coincidental.

Cover design by Erin Dameron-Hill (the miracle-worker)

ASIN: B0BSRDG3J7

Paperback: 9798374537338

Click here for a complete list of other works by Merry Farmer.

If you'd like to be the first to learn about when the next books in the series come out and more, please sign up for my newsletter here: http://eepurl.com/RQ-KX

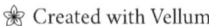 Created with Vellum

Dr. Todd Sullivan has worked hard against class and social expectations to secure a position as a physician at a prominent London hospital. This is his chance to rise above his station. But when he stumbles across a beaten and dying young man in the alley beside the hospital on his way to his first day of work, he incurs the wrath of hospital administrator, Dr. Keller, and is fired on the spot.

Todd has nowhere to go and no money to support himself or the injured mystery man.

Simon Warner thought he was dead and that an angel came to take him out of the misery of the world. But when he awakes and finds himself in the care of the very human Todd, he feels as though he has found heaven on earth. But thanks to him, Todd isn't safe. When they are evicted from Todd's flat, Simon must go from being the victim to the savior.

And when Simon realizes that the man who tried to kill him —and several other rent boys from Hyde Park—has a close connection to Todd, he finds himself turning to members of The Brotherhood to save them both.

Just a Little Prelude is a prequel novella to The Brotherhood series.

One

LONDON – JUNE, 1888

Dr. Todd Sullivan ducked and dodged through the busy morning shuffle of Oxford Street and along to Holborn, his heart in his throat. He had one hand clapped on his hat to keep it from being knocked off by the breeze or another pedestrian, and the other grasped around the handle of his medical bag, a smile on his face. The bag was old, its leather cracked, but to Todd, it was a symbol of everything he had worked for during the final, hectic years of his medical education. It wasn't much to look at—and neither was he, in his second-hand clothes and worn shoes—but it would accompany Todd to his first day of work at a real hospital.

St. Andrew's Hospital was nowhere near as grand as neighboring St. Bartholomew's, and it didn't even come close to having the history and grandeur of St. Thomas's on the Embankment, but it was a respected institution that cared for London's most desperate citizens, and, more importantly, it was the only hospital that had offered Todd a position as a surgeon. Todd wasn't one to question his blessings. He dodged around a pair of wan young ladies who looked to be shopgirls, tipping his hat in apology for nearly crashing headlong into them, then veered to the street corner so that he could cross.

It was something of a victory for him to have been hired at St. Andrew's at all. When he'd had his interview a fortnight ago, he'd arrived late, looking shabby and smelling of a pub. Never mind that his condition was because he'd stopped to help when a midday brawl at the Fox and Feathers burst into the street, leaving a few burly men—who had made his heart race for more than just their vigor as they threw punches and bloodied each other—in desperate need of patching up. The only things that had saved him from being tossed out of the interview were his exemplary marks and a letter of recommendation from the Royal College of Surgeons. But as the entire concept of attending formal schooling for medicine was a new one, Todd hadn't been certain that would be enough, and all for one, glaring reason.

"Pardon me, I'm so sorry," he murmured to a growling costermonger whose cart he nearly upset as he ducked around a corner close to St. Andrew's. One glance at his pocket watch had shown him that he was already in danger of being late, and not because of any pub brawls this time. He should have taken an omnibus from his pitiful room in Soho to reach the hospital on time, but he could barely afford his rent and a few, meager essentials, let alone daily fare for something as grand as an omnibus. Cutting through a back alley was his only hope of making a good impression by arriving on time for his first day of work. Heaven only knew he needed the money if he was going to keep his pitiful room or prevent himself from going hungry.

His lack of funds and his difficulty in finding a position at a hospital all came down to the same thing—his father, Dr.

George Sullivan. On the one hand, it was a point of pride for Todd to take up his father's profession and to treat the sick. On the other, his father's notorious incompetence and the number of patients he'd lost because of it was, as Todd discovered during his search for employment, notorious. Todd had always believed his father stopped practicing medicine and took up teaching because he had seen too much suffering and misery. It had come as a shock to him that his father had been pushed out of the profession after threats of prosecution from several families whose loved ones he had mistreated. In the end, his father's shame had inspired Todd to be the very best, most caring and compassionate, most well-regarded surgeon he could possibly—

His bolstering thoughts were cut short halfway down the dim and dank alley as he nearly stumbled over a prone form. His foot had made contact with whatever poor soul was crumpled on the damp stones in the middle of the passage, and the only way Todd would have recognized the pile of old rags as a person at all was because it moaned at the impact.

"I'm so sorry," Todd gasped, dropping immediately into a crouch. "I didn't see you there."

He spoke softly and rested a gentle hand on the form, rolling it over to assess what sort of misery he'd discovered. As it turned out, the poor, injured creature was a young man, barely more than a boy, his face swollen and bruised. The young man shivered and tried to hunch in on himself, but his strength was nearly gone. Todd sucked in a breath as he brushed the young man's hair back and moved a bit of the rags that passed for the lad's clothing only to find bruises—particularly around his throat—cuts, dried blood as well as blood that was still flowing, and soft, full lips that were split in more than one place.

"Oh, dear," Todd cooed in the most soothing voice he could manage. "You have had a bit of a tussle, haven't you?"

He brushed the man's hair back again, finding a cut along his hairline that was still oozing. He'd long since learned that the quieter and more confident he was with patients, the more they would trust him to treat them. It helped that he had a gentle nature to begin with—too gentle for his own good half the time. "Let's get you inside and see what we can do to patch you up," he said, shifting so that he could scoop the lad into his arms.

The young man groaned and protested, but he was far too weak to do anything to stop Todd from lifting him and settling him against his chest. Todd was deeply alarmed by how light and bony the lad was and how easy it was to carry him, even when he picked up his medical bag to carry in one hand. He proceeded carefully all the same, taking the young man around the corner to the front entrance of St. Andrew's.

"What has happened for me to find you in such a state, darling?" he asked the lad as he approached the front door. Immediately, Todd felt sheepish for addressing the patient with a term of endearment. He'd never been so sentimental with a patient before, but there was something about the way the young man leaned his head against Todd's shoulder, something in the feeling of abject misery the lad had, that went straight to Todd's heart. The young man didn't answer, so Todd continued in as cheery a voice as he could manage, "Don't you worry, I'll have you fixed up and as good as new in no time."

The hospital was bustling already as he carried the young man inside. So much so that none of the orderlies or nurses on duty took much notice of the two of them. The staff was too busy organizing the coughing, groaning, shivering ill who had come to the hospital for whatever treatment they needed. The sight of them filled Todd with a paradoxical thrill of excitement as he walked past them and down the hall that led to the examination rooms. He looked forward to finally being able to use the skills he'd worked so hard for to treat those who were in the deepest need.

He was glad that Dr. Keller, the hospital's head physician, had given him a tour of the building the day before. He was a surgeon and not a physician, so he wouldn't be working in that part of the hospital, but he knew just where to take the injured young man. But as he veered toward one of the examination rooms, a grey-haired nurse spotted him and attempted to step into his path.

"Excuse me, but where do you think you are going with that—" She gaped at the young man in Todd's arms, as if she wasn't certain he was even human.

"It's alright," Todd said, maintaining his calm. "I work here. I am Dr. Sullivan. I found this young man in the alley, and he is in desperate need of immediate attention."

"You cannot simply drag people in off the street and waste the hospital's resources on them," the nurse protested, jumping back as Todd moved around her.

"Is it not our duty to treat the sick and injured?" Todd asked her in return.

The nurse clucked and tutted, then turned to hurry off, muttering to herself. Todd ignored her. He set his medical bag aside and tried to lay the lad on the examination table in the small room, but the lad moaned and whimpered in protest, and weak though he was, he tried to fight Todd.

"Shh, shh," Todd attempted to soothe him. "It's alright. I'm just putting you down so that I can assess the damage and see to your wounds."

Less than a minute later, as Todd peeled back the threadbare shirt the young man wore and inched down his trousers, he thought he understood why the lad was so unwilling to let himself be examined. The injuries covering his torso and hips were extensive, and they seemed to be of a particular nature. The young man had clearly been beaten and handled roughly, but what caused Todd's throat to constrict and his blood to race through him in anger was the condition of his backside. The lad had been brutalized in a particularly heinous manner.

"There, there," Todd cooed to the young man as he left him to quickly gather all the supplies he would need to clean the lad's wounds and bandage the bits of him that needed it. From the state of the young man, there was a very real danger that infection could set in, which would have been far deadlier than any possible broken bones or flesh wounds that he might still uncover upon further examination. The lad was already feverish, which didn't bode well. "This might sting a bit, but it's all for the best, darling."

He would have shaken his head at himself for using the term of endearment again, except that a part of him felt like a young man who had been damaged in such a particular way probably needed all of the sweetness and compassion he could get. That and there were too many other things to focus on for Todd to question his choice of language.

He set to work cleaning the young man's wounds and examining him further. All of his other concerns faded away. Money didn't matter. His father's reputation was inconsequential. All Todd cared about was healing and soothing the young man in every way he could. He was forced to undress the lad entirely, which only unveiled a whole new set of horrors when he saw how malnourished and pale the lad was. If whatever attack he'd experienced hadn't killed him, there was a frightening possibility that hunger and deprivation would have done the job in short order. Todd found himself thinking that he wouldn't allow that to happen.

He was halfway through cleaning dirt out of the young man's cuts when a commotion in the hall caught his attention. A moment later, the nurse returned with Dr. Keller himself in tow.

"What is the meaning of this?" Dr. Keller boomed.

The young man flinched at Dr. Keller's shout. Todd had assumed the lad had passed out or fallen asleep while he was treating him, but with a burst of feeble strength, the lad pushed himself across the table, away from Dr. Keller and up against Todd, who reached for him to keep the young man from falling off the table entirely.

As soon as Dr. Keller saw the state of the lad, his eyes flared wide, but instead of the concern Todd expected from the head of the hospital, Dr. Keller boomed, "Who let this vermin into my hospital?"

Todd's eyes went wide in shock. "I found him in the alley outside the hospital on my way to work this morning," he explained. The young man continued his pitiful struggle to get away from Dr. Keller's disapproval, and in short order, Todd found himself clasping the lad to his chest to keep him from struggling and injuring himself more. "He is in a terrible state. Contusions, lacerations, and further injuries of a delicate nature." He glanced past Dr. Keller to the nurse, careful not to say anything a woman shouldn't hear.

"Get him out of here," Dr. Keller shouted, gesturing violently toward the door. "I won't have that sort of filth polluting my hospital."

Todd's heart dropped to his gut. "But he's in dire shape, sir," he protested. "He needs urgent medical attention. He won't survive without it."

"So?" Dr. Keller boomed. "Filth like that does not deserve to live. Get him out of here at once."

A heart-wrenching moan escaped from the young man, and Todd held him tighter. "This young man has been brutalized," he argued, drawing on all the strength he had to fight Dr. Keller. "Is it not our duty to treat the sick and injured, no matter who they are?"

"No," Dr. Keller insisted. "You know what he is, don't

you? You aren't so green and stupid that you can't tell a whore when you see one?"

The young man went slack in Todd's arms, and Todd had the uncomfortable feeling that he had passed out.

"It doesn't matter if he is a beggar or if he is the Prince of Wales," Todd insisted. "He has been beaten nearly to death, and he needs to be treated for his injuries."

Dr. Keller glowered, his face going red. He glanced briefly to the nurse, then took three, long steps across the room to glare at Todd over the examination table. "Are you disobeying a direct order from me?" he demanded. "And on your first day?"

Todd thought it was a tiny point in his favor that Dr. Keller remembered who he was. "Yes, I am, sir," he said, back straight, head held high. "My duty is to my patients, first and foremost."

Dr. Keller snorted. "Your duty is to me," he growled. "I hired you. I was the only one who would hire the son of that charlatan, George Sullivan. Do you think you'll ever be able to find another position in any hospital in London if you cross me, boy?"

Todd gulped, but stood his ground. "St. Andrew's isn't the only institution in need of trained medical staff," he said, clasping the young man to him tighter, more because he needed the comfort of his convictions than because the unconscious lad needed him.

Dr. Keller rocked back with a low, menacing laugh. "You think so? You think that the hospitals of London don't converse with each other, that I couldn't say one word and have you barred from every respectable medical practice in the city?"

Todd felt a shiver pass through him, but he would not back down. He couldn't. Not when a young man's life was at stake. "I have a duty of care to the sick and the injured," he said, meeting Dr. Keller's stare unflinchingly. "It doesn't matter who the patient is, only that he needs me."

For a brief moment, Todd thought that Dr. Keller had broken into a smile. He realized belatedly that it was no smile—it was a sneer of derision. "You'll learn the truth soon enough, Dr. Sullivan," he said in an ominously quiet voice. "You'll learn that some men are worthy of treatment and some are nothing but rubbish to be tossed on the midden heap. What remains to be seen is which sort you are."

Todd opened his mouth to protest that all men had value, but before he could get so much as a syllable out, Dr. Keller went on with, "Get out of my hospital now, sir."

Todd clamped his mouth shut, blinked several times, then asked, "I beg your pardon?"

"You heard me," Dr. Keller said, turning away. "You no longer have a position here. I'd say you are dismissed, but seeing as you never truly worked here, there is no need. You are trespassing on hospital property. I am calling an orderly to remove you."

He stormed out of the room before Todd could make a single sound of protest. The nurse tilted her nose up and *humphed* as if she agreed, then left as well.

For a few, stunned seconds, Todd merely stood there, clasping the unconscious young man to him. His mind didn't want to accept that everything he'd hoped and dreamed for had just crashed around him. He needed the job at St. Andrew's. He needed the money, but more than that, he needed to do what he had been born to do—he needed to be a healer.

Dr. Keller's distant call for an orderly to remove him set Todd in motion. He'd stripped the young man of all his clothes, and now he was loath to attempt to dress the lad in his dirty, probably lice-riddled things. Instead, he made a quick search of the examination room. There were no spare clothes available, but there were clean sheets in one cabinet. As fast as he could, Todd wrapped the young man in a sheet, then removed his coat—which he hadn't had time to remove when he entered the hospital—and tucked him into that. From there, he dashed around the room, filling his medical bag with bandages and a bottle of alcohol, one of iodine, and even a small bottle of aspirin. He had already been dismissed, and if he was going to be condemned, he might as well be condemned for theft as well. Chances were that the hospital wouldn't miss those few things.

Once he had the supplies closed up in his medical bag, he scooped the young man into his arms, grabbed his bag, and charged out into the hall. The hospital was already in a state —one which Todd hoped would allow him to rush out without being waylaid. He burst from the hall into the front room, praying that Dr. Keller, or whatever orderly he'd found to throw him out, wouldn't be there.

"Oy! Where do you think you're going?" one of the orderlies called after him as he neared the door.

Todd turned back to him only as long as it took to say, "You've no need to worry. I'm leaving, just as Dr. Keller has ordered. But shame on the lot of you for refusing to treat a desperately injured man, simply because he is poor." Perhaps it was beneath him to attempt to rile the people waiting to be seen in such a way, but the patients of St. Andrew's deserved to know that they could very well have been turned away in their hour of need, simply because of their class and misfortune.

The only effect of his words was that a sad-faced middle-aged man leapt up from the bench where he was sitting to hold the door open for Todd. Todd nodded in thanks to the man, then stepped out into the noise and drizzle of London.

As soon as he was outside, the too-light, still unconscious young man sagging against him, a wave of fear swept through Todd. He might have been trained as a surgeon, but unless he could find a position at a hospital, that wouldn't pay his rent or buy him food. He could just as easily have become a physician at a private practice on Harley Street, but not without a considerable amount of effort, and not immediately. The only action he could take in the here and now was to return to his rented room with the young man in his arms and make certain that the lad didn't die before nightfall.

Two

There was only one thought in Simon's head as he lay against the cold, hard stones of the alley, wracked with pain and delirious with fever. He didn't want to die alone. He'd spent almost his entire life alone, but to die that way seemed like insult added to so, so many injuries. He wanted to weep as the darkness of predawn gave way to the thin light of a dreary day, but he didn't have any tears left. Neither did he didn't have any words left. And as the city woke up and began to buzz around him, he wasn't certain how many breaths he had left either.

And then the angel came. Simon knew he was dead. The angel rolled him over and lifted him into his arms, carrying him up and up, but not quite so far as Heaven.

"What has happened for me to find you in such a state, darling?" the angel asked.

Simon couldn't answer. There was too much to be said. He wanted to leave it all behind and rest in the angel's embrace forever. He was so warm and soft, and he smelled of good things. Most of all, he held Simon, as if in answer to his prayer. He wouldn't die alone after all.

Sometime later, he wasn't certain how much, since time didn't seem to have meaning anymore, all of Simon's good, hopeful feelings were dashed. His angel was arguing with the Devil. Sudden terror filled Simon, and he did everything he could to get away from the Devil. He knew he didn't deserve it, he knew his life had been a wicked one, but it wasn't his fault. Perhaps his angel could save him. His angel wouldn't let the Devil drag him down to Hell. In fact, his angel seemed to scoop him into his arms and hold him close, as if he would fight with his last breath to take Simon to Heaven instead of letting him go to Hell, like he deserved.

And then everything was ruined.

"You know what he is, don't you? You aren't so green and stupid that you can't tell a whore when you see one?" the Devil demanded of his angel.

Simon wanted to cry out in despair and weep until he was out of tears and turned into nothing but raindrops. His angel knew the truth now. There was no chance of him making it to Heaven. The Devil would surely take him now. The thought filled him with such desolation that he passed out, retreating into the darkness.

But when he awoke, his angel was still there and the Devil was not.

"That's it, darling," his angel said in soft, gossamer tones. "Drink a little more."

Simon's angel held something to his lips, tipping it so that warm, bitter liquid seeped into his mouth, coating his tongue. More than that, he became aware that he was lying in a bed with cool, soft sheets and not on the stones of a London alley. He was too afraid still to open his eyes so that he could be sure, but wherever he was now, it was quiet, and it was safe.

"A little more," his angel coaxed. "Just a bit. It will make you feel better, I promise."

Simon tensed. He'd been made the same promise before when a man he'd been sent to entertain had plied him with wine or spirits. The stuff that his angel wanted him to drink didn't taste like that, though. And if drinking for him meant that his angel would take him to Heaven, then he would drink.

"That's it. Very good," his angel cooed, then stroked Simon's head when he took the cup away. His angel sighed, then said, "What am I going to do with you?"

Simon wanted to beg him not to leave, to take him along wherever angels went. He would have done anything for him, anything at all, if it meant he could be safe and no longer alone.

"Rest now," his angel said, and of all things, Simon thought he felt warm lips on his forehead. "Rest and heal. I'm off to the pawn shop. Let's hope they give me a good price for this watch, because it's all I have left. I'll be home soon."

Simon did as he was ordered to do. He always did what he was ordered to do, whether he wanted it or not. Except this time, he didn't feel bad about it. His angel was going to take him to Heaven.

When next he woke—he wasn't certain how much time had passed—Simon realized the truth. He was not in Heaven. He was not dead at all. He was in a bed that appeared to be in a small, neat, sparsely-decorated room. For the first time in what felt like a while, when Simon opened his eyes, he noticed his surroundings. The afternoon sun peeked through threadbare curtains on the room's single window. Aside from the narrow bed where he lay, the room had only a wardrobe, a small, squat stove, and a table with two chairs. There wasn't even a carpet on the floor. There was, however, a kettle steaming on the stove, and the faint scent of bread filled the air.

Simon used every bit of strength he had to push himself up. He was surprised to see that he wore a nightshirt, though it was too big for him. He was also surprised to find pillows under his head. He was able to shift so that he sat against them, not fully upright, but enough to get a better look at the room. There were books and a strange, old bag on the table. Simon was more interested in the steaming kettle and the loaf of bread and glass jar of what looked like broth on the far end of the table. His stomach twinged longingly for the bread, but he knew he would never have the strength to reach it.

A pinch of despair shot through him, but seconds later, it turned to abject fear as a voice sounded in the hall and the door handle rattled.

"Yes, Mrs. Frampton," the voice of his angel sounded through the door. "I'm sorry Mrs. Frampton. I know it's late, but I will pay you as soon as I'm able." Simon heard a woman's voice farther down the hall, then his angel repeated, "Yes, Mrs. Frampton," as the door cracked open.

Twin feelings of fear and elation filled Simon as the door opened halfway and his angel slipped in—almost as though he didn't want anyone on the other side of the door to see him entering the room. His angel shut the door behind him and let out a heavy breath. A moment later, his angel turned, found Simon partially sitting up and staring at him, and burst into a smile that was so beautiful it nearly made Simon weep.

"You're awake," his angel said, striding across the room. He held a small sack which he deposited on the table before coming to the side of the bed and sitting.

Simon panicked. He wasn't dead, so his angel wasn't really an angel. But he still seemed like one, and Simon had no idea how to converse with an angel.

"Your color is looking quite good today," his angel said, reaching out a hand and laying it on Simon's forehead. "And your fever is most definitely gone."

Simon couldn't breathe. The touch of his angel's hand was soft and gentle. He nearly groaned at how good it felt, but swallowed the sound before his angel could take it the wrong way. Or before his angel could see right through him to tell how much Simon wanted to feel that touch all over his body. It was wicked of him, yes, but he didn't want it for wicked reasons, he just wanted to be loved. In the good way.

"Are you hungry?" his angel asked, getting up and crossing to the table. He opened the sack he'd brought home and took out what looked like two sweet buns filled with raisins or some other dried fruit.

Again, Simon nearly groaned with want. Tears filled his eyes as his angel brought one of the buns back to the bed. As he sat, he tore off a small piece and handed it to Simon.

"Go easy to start," he said. "It's been days since I found you, and who knows how long it was before that when you last ate."

Simon nearly dropped the bit of bun as he raised it to his mouth. "Days?" he croaked.

His angel burst into a beautiful smile. "So you *can* speak."

He was far and away the most beautiful man Simon had ever seen. He was young, probably only a few years older than Simon himself, but there was a sort of kindness and seriousness about him that made him appear refined and handsome. He had warm, brown eyes and soft brown hair that Simon immediately wanted to touch. His jaw was square and his mouth curved into a smile. His angel had broad shoulders and a slender build as well, and Simon remembered what it had felt like to be held in the man's arms.

"Or perhaps not?" his angel asked with a teasing glint in his eyes.

"I...I can speak," Simon said, lowering his head bashfully and nibbling on the bit of bun he'd been given. It was the most delicious thing he'd ever tasted.

"Good, I'm glad," his angel said. He watched Simon eat for a moment before asking, "What is your name?"

Simon swallowed, regretting how dry his throat was, but too afraid to ask for something to drink, and croaked, "Simon."

"Simon," his angel repeated with a smile. "My name is Todd."

Simon stared at his angel. He couldn't possibly call him by his given name. His angel was too far above him for that. He avoided the conundrum by eating more of his bun.

"Are you hungry?" Todd asked him. "Perhaps thirsty?"

Simon nodded.

"Let me fix you some tea, then." He stood, and immediately Simon missed his presence. "Tea makes everything better," Todd said as he moved to the stove.

Simon watched his angel intently as he poured water from the kettle into a small, chipped teapot, then took it to the table to steep. He fetched a battered, tin cup from a small shelf beside the stove, took the tiniest sugar lump Simon had ever seen from a small bowl on the shelf, and brought a narrow pitcher that couldn't have contained more than a swallow of milk to the table and set to work preparing tea.

"H-how long have I been here?" Simon dared to ask, trembling at his own boldness.

"It's been four days," Todd answered. He kept his smile in place as he brought the tea to the bed, but Simon thought there was something tight and worried in his angel's eyes. "I wasn't certain you were going to make it that first day, but you're a fighter."

A swoop of dread filled Simon's gut. He was not a fighter. That was why he'd been so popular. He never fought anyone, no matter what they wanted to do. He couldn't bear to tell Todd that, so he took the cup of tea from him and sipped it as an excuse not to say more.

It was the best tea he'd ever tasted. He drank it fast—too fast, as it turned out, which caused him to cough and sputter.

"Slowly," Todd told him, pulling the cup away from his mouth. "You'll need to go slowly at first. Your stomach is not ready for you to eat too swiftly yet."

Simon nodded and did as his angel asked, sipping from the cup instead of gulping. He watched Todd over the cup's brim, marveling at how beautiful he was and how he'd saved him.

"You'd been severely abused when I found you," Todd said in a careful voice, watching Simon's lips for a moment instead of looking him in the eye. "Do you remember how that happened?"

Simon hid his shame and confusion by tilting the cup up higher, as if he could hide behind it. He shook his head, but the truth was, he could remember exactly what had happened. He'd been in the park with the others. They'd watched the gentlemen cruising. Some of the others had picked their marks, and some, like Simon, had waited to be chosen. And he was chosen. The gentleman had frightened him from the start, but he offered more money than Simon usually got. He'd taken Simon away in a carriage—which should have been a warning sign—and had him do all the usual things. But that hadn't been enough. He'd fucked Simon brutally, then hit him and strangled him and ordered him never to tell a soul what they'd done. Then he'd thrown him out of the carriage and into the alley. He'd been supposed to die.

"I take it that wasn't the first time you'd found yourself in that sort of desperate situation?" his angel asked.

The question pierced right to Simon's heart, and in spite

of the tea and bun, he burst into tears. "I'm sorry," he said. "You don't want someone like me here. I'll…I'll go." He tried to push the bedclothes aside and swing his legs around, but he was too weak.

"No!" Todd laid a steadying hand on Simon's leg, keeping him where he was. Simon felt his touch as though it were lightning. "No, stay where you are. I do want you here. I brought you here so I could take care of you."

Simon glanced at his angel with watery eyes. No one had ever said anything so kind to him in his life. He didn't have the first clue what he could say in return, which only caused him to burst into tears.

"Shh, shh," Todd shushed him, taking the cup of tea out of his hand and setting it on the rickety table beside the bed. He scooted closer and closed his arms around Simon, drawing him against his chest. "I don't care who you are, it is my responsibility to care for you until you are fully healed."

Simon continued to weep against his angel's shoulder. If that were the case, he hoped he never healed. No one had ever taken care of him or treated him with even a shred of kindness.

"I've been monitoring your injuries closely," Todd went on after a few minutes of the two of them just sitting still. "Your fever broke two days ago, which is a very good sign. It means you did not suffer a devastating infection, as I feared you might, considering how dirty you were."

Simon shrank away from him in shame, hiding his face.

"It wasn't your fault," Todd stressed. "I suspect you haven't been living in the best of conditions. Am I right?"

Simon peeked up at him, then nodded. "Me and some other lads live rough in Hyde Park," he confessed. "We look out for each other, and we do what we have to in order to survive."

Todd let out a breath. "It is as I suspected." He paused, then asked, "Do you have any family?"

Simon shook his head. He could barely remember his mother. She'd dropped him at an orphanage when he was small. The orphanage had fed and clothed him, but he would never have called them family.

"Just your Hyde Park friends, then?" Todd asked on.

Simon nodded. Even those bonds were more out of necessity than real attachment. It was dangerous to become attached to lads who might disappear without a trace at any moment.

"How have you—"

That was as far as Todd got before the door to his room flew open and a dowdy, middle-aged woman whose hair was coming out of the tight bun on her head barged in, saying, "I've asked Mr. Frampton, but he says he cannot—" She stopped mid-sentence and gaped at Simon. Her expression quickly turned furious. "What is the meaning of this?" she demanded, her voice an octave higher.

Todd leapt off the bed and took a few steps toward the woman. "I can explain," he said, a desperate flush coming to his face, his eyes wide. "Simon is a patient. I found him battered and broken and close to death last week, just outside the hospital."

"Then why isn't he in the hospital now?" Mrs. Frampton demanded, angrier still.

"The hospital turned him away," Todd said. "I had no choice but to bring him back here to treat him. Otherwise, he would have died."

Details rushed back to Simon. His angel had taken him inside the hospital where he'd been dumped. He'd tried to treat him there, but they'd been chased out.

"Dr. Sullivan," Mrs. Frampton said, glaring at Todd,

planting her fists on her hips, "this is not an infirmary. It's not a charity ward either. Your rent is past due, and you've taken it upon yourself to treat patients here?"

"Not patients, just Simon," Todd attempted to explain.

"Is he paying you?" Mrs. Frampton demanded. "Because Mr. Frampton wants his rent money by the end of the week, or out you go."

"I will get that money to you as soon as I can, madam, I promise," Todd said.

Simon writhed with guilt. He glanced to the half-eaten roll in his lap, the tea and broth on the table, and the loaf of bread. Doctor or not, Simon knew the signs of a man without money. He had a horrible feeling that the little Todd did have had just been spent on treats for him.

Mrs. Frampton eyed Todd suspiciously, then narrowed her eyes at Simon. "You'd better pay up in full by Friday," she said in a thin voice. "Mr. Frampton is mighty fractious when he doesn't get his rent money."

"I understand, madam," Todd said with a bow. "You will get your money."

Mrs. Frampton glared at Todd, then backed into the hall. She shut the door behind her with a clatter. Todd let out a heavy breath, his shoulders drooping. Then he turned back to the bed. The worried look he sent Simon was enough to break what little heart Simon had.

Paradoxically, Todd said, "Don't worry," as he came back to the bed and sat by Simon's side once again. "I'm searching for another position with a hospital. In the meantime, I'm certain I'll be able to pick up a day job here or there. And I won't turn you out. I won't abandon you as long as you still need me."

It was too much for Simon to bear. "Let me pay you," he squeaked, moving the half roll aside and scooting toward

Todd. Already, he felt better, stronger. If not because of the food, then because he knew what he had to do. "It's not much, but it is payment of a sort."

Face flushing, he reached for the fastenings of Todd's trousers. It was very possibly the first time in his life when he had ever looked forward to servicing a man.

But no sooner had his thin, pale hands skated near Todd's trousers than his angel caught them and pushed them aside with a loud, "No!"

Simon gulped in fear. The emotion quickly turned to despair. "Don't you like me?" he asked in a tiny voice, wracked with shame. He'd been so certain that he'd seen want in his angel's eyes when he'd looked at him.

Todd let out a breath, taking both of Simon's hands in his. "You don't have to do those things out of any obligation to me," he explained, not looking Simon in the eyes. "I ask for nothing in return for healing you."

Simon swallowed hard. "But don't you enjoy it?"

Todd's face flooded with red. "I don't know."

Simon blinked at him. "How don't you know?"

Todd writhed and turned even redder. "I've...never... done anything like that," he finished in a rush.

Simon tried not to gape at him. Todd was beautiful, he was kind, and he was older than Simon's twenty years, but he hadn't done *anything* before? It was a situation Simon absolutely did not know how to deal with.

"More tea, I think," Todd said in an overly cheerful voice, standing and moving to the table without looking at Simon. "And then perhaps I'll heat some soup."

Simon noticed that Todd's trousers didn't lay as flat as they had when he'd first sat down, but that only puzzled him. As far as he was concerned, Todd could have him in every way that it was possible for him to be had. He would give his angel everything.

But as he settled against his pillows again and reached for the bun to finish eating it, a darker thought occurred to Simon. His angel needed so much more than pleasure. He needed money. Simon had to find a way to help him as repayment for saving his life.

Three

The next week was perhaps the strangest of Todd's life. The entire world seemed to be against him. Every hospital and physician's practice in London that he appealed to refused to interview him, let alone hire him. Even some of the charity hospitals that he would have thought would be desperate for a trained surgeon slammed their doors on him. The only work he was able to get in order to put food on the table and pay for new clothing for Simon was manual day labor. Not only wasn't he strong enough to be asked back, he was so concerned about injuring his hands—the tools of his chosen trade—that it made him surprisingly inept at the jobs he got.

At the same time, every moment he spent at home with Simon was wonderful. The young man was timid and quiet. He only spoke when Todd asked him direct questions and he was reticent about saying anything about his life. But the light in his smile when he listened to the rambling stories Todd told made Todd feel like he could conquer the world. And in short order, Todd felt that if he ever did conquer the world, he would wrap it up in ribbons and hand it to Simon as a gift from his heart. He would have done anything for the young man, anything at all. And Todd was certain beyond a doubt that Simon would have done anything for him. *Anything.*

Those thoughts and the physical and emotional feelings that came with them were strange and difficult for Todd to manage, particularly as the two of them began to share the same bed once Simon had recovered a bit. Just over a week after his confrontation with Mrs. Frampton, after Simon had made an advance on him that had both shocked and intrigued him, Todd was pulsing with so much restless energy that it woke him in the early hours of dawn. He drew in a sharp breath as he realized he'd drawn Simon's back to his chest in his sleep and that he held the young man like a lover. Even more alarming, his morning tumescence seemed to delight over how perfectly it fit against the sensual curve of Simon's backside.

Even though he had just awakened, Todd's senses heightened. He breathed in Simon's scent—a combination of soap and sweat, since he'd bathed the night before. He slowly lifted himself so that he could rest on one arm and gaze down at Simon's still-sleeping form. Simon looked so much healthier now than he had when Todd had stumbled across him in the alley. Simon was still slight and sylph-like, but his cheeks were rosy and had filled out a bit. Todd was seized with the mad notion that he wanted to press his lips to the softness of those cheeks, or better still, taste Simon's full, pink lips.

That thought sent a jolt of lust through Todd that unnerved him in the extreme. He wasn't the sort of man to take advantage of someone who was as helpless as Simon was. But he would be lying to himself if he said he didn't want Simon desperately. Long ago, he'd reconciled himself to the belief that he would never have what he wanted because it was unseemly and forbidden. The effects of those inclinations were what had driven the wedge between him and his father—indirectly, of course; his family didn't know he fancied men—and why he wasn't welcome in his own family's home anymore. He'd never acted on those impulses, though. Not once.

But now, with Simon slumbering away, so soft and sweet, with his delicate body clothed only in Todd's old nightshirt as he pressed against him, Todd was tempted as he never had been before. He smiled down at Simon, moving carefully to brush a lock of the young man's blond hair back from his face. He didn't stop there. Holding his breath, Todd traced his fingers over Simon's warm cheek, touching his lips lightly, desperate not to wake Simon. The top few buttons of the nightshirt had come undone, and with a daring that Todd didn't know he possessed, he brushed his fingers over Simon's delicate collarbone and across the top of his chest. Simon had barely any hair on his body and had only needed to shave once in the fortnight that he'd been with Todd, which only made Todd want to touch him more. Simon's one exposed nipple seemed to call out to him, begging to be caressed.

Todd nearly gave in to that temptation, but Simon drew in a breath and stretched, waking up. The way the young man moved his body caused him to rub against Todd's erection, and it brought Todd so close to unmanning himself that it was all he could do to stifle a groan. Hiding the way Simon made him feel seemed next to impossible as the young man rolled to his back, opened his blue eyes, and smiled up at Todd as though he were the sun and the stars combined.

"I like it when you touch me," Simon murmured, still groggy with sleep.

It was too much. Todd's cock throbbed and his balls felt heavy and tight, but in spite of the unspoken invitation, he couldn't importune someone who was under his care that way. Instead, he rolled to his other side and slipped quickly out of the bed, careful to keep his pronounced erection—which was desperately obvious through the thin fabric of his nightshirt—away from Simon's view.

"Good morning," he called over his shoulder as he hurried to the screen in the far corner of the room, behind which sat his chamber pot. "Give me just a moment and I'll make some tea."

He ducked behind the screen—which he'd picked from a rubbish heap during his search for employment when he realized Simon might like the privacy it afforded—and lifted his nightshirt to take hold of his cock. The quickest way to bring himself to a more presentable state was to come, which he did with embarrassing speed. There was something lowering about not having the self-control to master his body when he was with Simon, but also something sweet and delightful about having that sort of a response to the beautiful young man.

As soon as he felt he was in control of himself, he slipped back around the screen and headed straight for the stove to rekindle its fire. Simon had risen from bed and was now attempting to make the bed, though it was clear to Todd that he'd never been taught how to do so properly.

"Thank you," he said all the same. "You don't have to do that, though. You're still recovering."

"I feel much stronger," Simon insisted, turning to Todd with a smile.

"I still think you should rest," Todd said, setting the kettle on the stove once the fire was going, then moving to the washstand. "I need to set out early if I'm to make it all the way to Kensington to search for a position, but I want you to continue to convalesce until I'm certain you've healed."

"Yes, Todd," Simon said softly. The pure obedience in his

voice sent shivers down Todd's spine. It was no wonder that the lad had found himself in such dire circumstances. His disposition was so gentle and accommodating that Todd found himself wondering how he'd survived in rough surroundings as long as he had.

He finished washing and dressing, then joined Simon at the table as the kettle began to steam. It would be a while still before the water was hot enough for tea, but Todd didn't think he could stay in the room with Simon for that long without embarrassing both of them.

"You know how to make tea?" he asked, gazing down at Simon as he stood beside the lad's chair.

Simon nodded as he stared up at Todd with adoring eyes.

"Good." Todd risked squeezing Simon's shoulder. The young man was still bony, but he'd gained a bit of weight since Todd had taken him under his wing. The trouble was, every improvement Simon made had Todd wanting to keep him close instead of letting him return to his old life. He pulled his hand away reluctantly and said, "I need to check with the hospital I inquired at the other day to see if they are hiring," he said, though it was a bit of a lie, since no hospital had allowed him to inquire in the first place in more than a week. "I'll be back soon, hopefully with good news."

Simon's expression dropped. "Do you truly have to go?" he asked in a voice that came close to melting Todd's heart.

"I'm afraid so," Todd said, trying to smile. "Employment is necessary." And if he didn't leave and give himself time to settle, it was as like as not that the two of them would end up back in bed. As much as it pained him to admit, he didn't know the first thing about what to do with a man in bed, and chances were that he would only embarrass both of them.

He marched to the door, grabbing his jacket from its peg. "I'll return as soon as I can," he said, then all but fled the room before he changed his mind and flew to Simon.

Simon's quiet call of, "Goodbye," tugged at Todd's heart. Simon clearly didn't want him to go, but he had to.

As quickly as he could, Todd raced down the stairs to leave the boarding house. He had to find a position at a hospital immediately. He needed the money, and he needed the security a position would provide. He needed to be able to continue to care for Simon. The idea of the delicate young man fending for himself in the cruel world of London—a world that had nearly killed him once already—was too much for Todd to bear. There was no doubt in Todd's mind that if Simon were turned out, he'd end up right back where he'd started, and Todd couldn't bear the thought.

"And just where do you think you're going?" the gruff voice of Mr. Frampton stopped Todd as he pulled open the boarding house door.

"To look for work," Todd explained to the man, fighting desperately to maintain his dignity.

Mr. Frampton narrowed his eyes and stalked closer to him. He was a thick-set, swarthy man with little imagination, and the few encounters Todd had had with the man hadn't been pleasant. "Your rent is fifteen days past due," Frampton grumbled.

"I should have it by the end of the week," Todd said, knowing full well he'd said the same thing the week before and failed to deliver.

"And why should I believe you?" Frampton asked, his eyes narrowing.

"I am a man of my word," Todd said.

Frampton merely grunted. He continued to stare at Todd, as if he expected something from him.

"I need to go now," Todd said, ashamed of how thin his voice sounded. "Good day to you, Mr. Frampton."

He rushed out of the boarding house and into the street, an uneasy feeling making its way through him. Frampton wasn't the sort to do something drastic. The man didn't have the imagination for menace the way some other men did. That was the one thing that had saved Todd from being tossed out in the street before. But that didn't mean the man would be patient forever.

In spite of his hopes and desperation, the results of his morning's search for employment were as fruitless as they'd been for the past fortnight. True to Dr. Keller's prediction, not a single institution was willing to interview him once he gave his name. But time was running out, and Todd needed to do something.

Which was how he found himself in a small chemist's shop near Kensington.

"Might you have any position at all open?" he asked the chemist working behind the counter. "I am a trained surgeon. I've studied with the Royal College of Surgeons. I could learn to know my way around a chemist's shop."

"Why would a surgeon want to work for a chemist?" the shop's owner asked, narrowing his eyes with the same sort of suspicion Todd had found at every turn of late.

A patron standing at the counter—one of the most striking and beautiful men Todd had ever seen—seemed equally curious about Todd's answer.

"I have attempted to secure a position at a hospital," Todd answered judiciously, "but due to a disagreement with the administrator of St. Andrew's Hospital, I've found that few institutions will consider me."

"Is that so?" the handsome patron asked. His voice was as smooth as silk, and to Todd's surprise, he didn't even try to hide his fey mannerisms.

Todd studied the man briefly, drawn in by the juxtaposition of gentility and power that the man possessed. He was obviously of a Uranian disposition, but rather than try to hide it, as Todd did, he seemed to wear it like the finely-tailored suit he was dressed in. "It is," Todd answered him.

"And none of these other institutions will so much as speak to you?" the stranger asked.

Todd didn't understand what interest it was to the man, but he answered all the same with, "Not a one. I…I suspect some sort of collusion on the part of hospital administrators."

"What a delightful challenge." The stranger burst into a smile. He held out his hand and announced, "Lionel Mercer, at your service."

Startled, Todd took Mr. Mercer's hand. "Dr. Todd Sullivan," he introduced himself.

Mercer narrowed his eyes a bit, assessing Todd in a way that made him feel as though Mercer could see right into his soul. He drew Todd to one side so that the chemist could serve another customer and asked, "What was the nature of this disagreement at St. Andrew's?"

In spite of the desperate self-consciousness Mercer raised in him, Todd answered, "I found a young man that had been beaten nearly to death in the alley outside of the hospital and brought him inside to treat the lad. Dr. Keller discovered us, and when he ordered me to abandon the young man, I refused. He did not want a whore treated in his hospital, but I insisted we had a duty of care. So Dr. Keller threw us both out."

Mercer's eyebrows rose to his hairline. "How dare the man?"

As nice as it was for Todd to have someone share his opinion of the situation, he wasn't in a mood to stand around gossiping about it. "He was the hospital administrator. And it appears he has clout with the other hospitals. As a result, I've found myself and my patient, Simon, in a desperate situation."

Mercer looked even more surprised. "You still have the battered man with you?"

Todd nodded, blushing hot. "He has made a fine recovery, though."

For whatever reason, that bit of information seemed to have struck a chord with Mercer, spurring him to action. He reached into the interior pocket of his jacket and pulled out a card, which he handed to Todd. "Perhaps I could be of some assistance. If you have further trouble finding suitable employment, please do call on me at this address. I have a knack for helping people out of sticky situations, particularly our sort of people."

Desperate, bristling self-consciousness slithered through Todd. If Mercer could tell at a glance that the two of them had specific similarities, then who else could tell? If it was that obvious, he might never find employment again.

He stared down at the card. It was for the Law Offices of Dandie & Wirth, which didn't seem to make sense. He wasn't in need of a solicitor, he was in need of employment.

"I can help you," Mercer insisted. "You will see. Call as soon as possible."

He stepped away from Todd and back to the chemist's counter. Todd turned to hurry out of the shop. He'd never gotten an answer about a position there, but the conversation with Mercer had left him unsettled for several reasons, and he needed a breath of fresh air to clear his head.

In spite of his intent to keep searching for employment, his feet took him right back to the boarding house. Or perhaps it would have been more accurate to say that his heart took him back to Simon. He needed to be around the young man's bright, soothing presence to make sense of the strange encounter with Mr. Mercer.

As soon as he set foot through the door and into his

rooms, though, his heart burst with affection for an entirely different reason.

Simon gasped and turned away from the open wardrobe, where he appeared to be in the process of folding and organizing Todd's meager amount of clothing. The room was spotless, as if it had been scrubbed from top to bottom and put in perfect order.

"Todd," Simon gasped, breaking into a wide smile and stepping away from the wardrobe. "I didn't expect you home until after lunch. Does this mean you found a position?"

So many things in the way Simon spoke and looked pierced straight to Todd's heart. He strode immediately across the room to the young man, stopping just short of letting himself embrace Simon and kiss him with the full emotion of his heart and soul.

"Not yet," he said, then went straight on to, "You've been busy."

Simon sent him a bashful look that had Todd's heart racing and his cock hardening. "I needed to do something," he explained. "I'm well enough now that staying in bed is a chore. I figured that if I tidied up, you would be pleased."

"I am pleased, Simon," Todd said. "More pleased than you could know. Thank you."

He didn't have anything more to say, but he couldn't pull his eyes away from Simon or move apart from him. Simon seemed perfectly content merely to gaze up at Todd in adoration, his huge, generous, fragile heart on his sleeve. It was more than Todd could bear. Against his better judgement, but fully in line with his heart, he closed his hands on either side of Simon's face and tilted it up for a kiss. Simon gasped slightly as their lips met, then gave in completely and moaned with pleasure.

The sound was like setting a spark to dry kindling. Todd didn't have the first idea of how to properly kiss a man, but that didn't stop him from stepping into Simon and circling one arm around him. He let nature take over and pressed his mouth to Simon's. Simon, on the other hand, knew exactly what he was doing and deepened their kiss. He parted Todd's lips and explored him with his tongue, but in a way that still felt submissive and sweet. It increased Todd's confidence and inspired him to kiss Simon more deeply.

Todd was on the verge of losing himself completely when the door flew open, banging so hard against the wall that it sounded like a gunshot. Todd and Simon gasped and leapt apart, and Todd turned to find Frampton standing in the doorway, looking both furious and disgusted.

"What in the bloody hell is this?" Frampton demanded. He didn't wait for an answer. He rushed straight on with, "I won't have any of this in my house. Get out, both of you. Out now! I'm calling the police to have you both arrested for indecency."

They were the words that every man like them dreaded to hear, and even though Frampton left the room to storm down the hall, Todd felt as though the situation was even more dangerous than if Frampton had attacked them.

"Hurry," he hissed at Simon, lunging toward his wardrobe and reaching for the suitcase on the top shelf. "He really will call the police. We have to leave, now."

Four

Simon whimpered and scampered around the room, gathering up as much as he could of Todd's belongings to throw into the suitcase. His heart couldn't decide if it wanted to soar with joy over the way Todd had finally kissed him or sink into the pit of his stomach because they had been caught. Either way, an odd sort of confidence filled him. He'd been in this situation before. He knew what was necessary to flee before the police came. Unless there was a bobby right outside on the street—and the area where Todd lived wasn't the sort where coppers prowled during daylight hours—they had a good twenty minutes before anyone would come for them.

"It's a good thing I barely have anything left to my name," Todd said with a feeble attempt to laugh the situation off as he closed the lid of his suitcase and buckled it shut. "That makes it easier to run. Come on."

He reached out a hand for Simon as he headed toward the door. It was an endearing gesture—one that Todd couldn't possibly know the significance of. For the first time in his life, Simon wasn't being discarded, shoved aside, or left behind. Todd wanted him to flee with him. He wanted Simon to be safe.

Simon rushed for him, grasping his hand and dashing into the hall and down the stairs with him. Todd had kept him safe and made him well in so many ways in the past fortnight. He had found clothes and shoes for Simon, fed him, bound his wounds, and held him at night, when nightmares had threatened. Simon wasn't ignorant enough to miss the fact that Todd was struggling, though he didn't understand why a doctor couldn't find a position at a hospital. Whatever the case was, Simon felt a deep sense of purpose that went all the way to his bones. As they hurried out into the street, hand in hand, running to get as far away from the boarding house as possible before the police arrived, Simon felt as though the time had finally come when he could repay Todd's kindness in a way that would mean something.

They stopped running once they reached Oxford Street and the heavy, midday traffic it held. There was no better place to lose oneself and to stay hidden than in a crowd. But before they had made it to the end of the street, Todd began to flag. Still catching his breath, he clapped a hand to his hat and turned this way and that, as if searching for something, with a suddenly desperate look.

"Where do we go?" he asked with more uncertainty in his eyes than Simon wanted to see.

As much as it pained Simon to see his angel at a loss, every fiber of his being thrilled at the prospect of being able to be of real use to Todd.

"I know," he said, starting forward along Oxford Street, heading west, determination in his steps. "I know where we can go."

Todd followed him, which filled Simon with even more confidence. It meant that his angel trusted him, even though he was a nobody who had lived most of his life on the streets.

He didn't feel like that miserable whore he'd been just over a fortnight ago. He wasn't certain who or what he felt that he was now, but it wasn't that desperate and abused rent-boy.

He led Todd down Oxford Street to Cumberland Gate, passing through Marble Arch and into Hyde Park. It seemed almost laughable how Todd glanced around in wonder at the massive structure, then gaped at everything there was to see in Hyde Park. Someone was delivering some sort of a speech, as usual, at Speaker's Corner, and for a moment Simon considered stopping so that Todd could listen to them.

"Have you never been to Hyde Park before?" Simon asked as he gestured for Todd to follow him along some of the lesser-traveled paths, toward the far end of the park, where the shrubs and trees grew closer together and more respectable people stayed away.

"I'm a Londoner," Todd said. "Of course I have." But from the way he glanced around at the variety of sights and people crowding the park in the middle of a pretty, June day, Simon wondered if he truly had. "We didn't come that often," Todd admitted a moment later, seeming to shake himself out of his wonder and focus more on Simon. "My father believed leisure was the Devil's handiwork. And later, after the disgrace, he didn't like to show his face in public."

Simon's brow shot up, and he nearly missed a step. "What disgrace?"

Todd's face colored. They dodged around a trio of nannies pushing prams and turned down an even narrower side path before he answered with, "My father was also a doctor, a physician, but he was drummed out of medical practice after a series of lawsuits against him for incompetence."

"Was he incompetent?" Simon asked. For all the talking Todd had done to entertain him for the past fortnight, he hadn't said much about his family. Simon would have doubted that Todd even had a family, except that he'd mentioned his father, mother, and siblings in passing.

Todd sighed as they slowed their steps. "He was," he admitted. "He caused more harm than good. People died because of his mistakes. I didn't realize what was going on at first. I thought my father left medicine to become a teacher for other reasons. It was only much later, when we had a certain…disagreement over a young lady, that he spilled the truth to me. Settling the lawsuits bankrupted him, which is why I haven't sought my family's help these past two weeks."

The awkward silence that followed Todd's admission made Simon think there were other reasons he hadn't sought his family's help on top of that, but it wasn't his place to ask. He didn't like the implication that a young lady had been involved.

"I had such high hopes that succeeding as a surgeon could somehow redeem him," Todd mumbled, mostly to himself. He shook his head, then seemed to push the whole thing aside. He glanced to Simon, smiled, and asked, "Is this where you spent your time before…." He blushed rather than finishing his sentence.

"It's where I lived," Simon admitted in a whisper, then glanced around quickly to make certain there were no bobbies around to overhear.

"The police allowed you to live in Hyde Park?" Todd asked, far too loud.

Before Simon could answer, a call of, "Simon, is that you?" sounded from a shady patch close to a thick cluster of bushes.

Simon didn't know whether to smile or panic. His whole body seemed to vibrate with anxious anticipation as he turned to discover who was calling out to him. He breathed a sigh of relief a moment later when he spotted his friend

Robbie standing with two other young men—Oliver and a new boy that Simon didn't know—to wave to him.

"They're safe," Simon reassured Todd, touching his hand before stepping off the path and walking across the grass to the shady patch. "Alright, Robbie," he greeted his friend, nodding to the other two.

"We thought you were done for," Oliver said, standing as well. He helped the other boy to stand, but the lad was slow to get to his feet. He was wan and sickly, and judging by the way he favored one side, he was in pain.

"I thought I was done for too," Simon told the others. "But Dr. Sullivan found me and saved me." He beamed at Todd, surprised—as he had been over and over—by how deep the adoration he felt for the man reached within him.

Todd wore a frown, though. Unsurprisingly, he'd noticed something was wrong with the new boy immediately. "Are you well, son?" he asked, stepping closer to the boy and setting his suitcase down. Todd was only twenty-five, as Simon had learned in the past fortnight, which made him only a few years older than most of the boys in the park, but it felt right for him to refer to the new boy as "son".

"He had a bad time of it last night," Robbie explained, his tone suspicious. He threw an arm around the new boy's shoulder and pulled him closer. "It's no concern of yours."

Simon flushed hot with embarrassment at his friend's behavior. "Dr. Sullivan is a doctor," he whispered, as if that were all the explanation needed.

"Yeah?" Robbie asked, his chin tilted up. "So was the bloke what broke Freddy's arm last month."

Simon's face heated even more. "Dr. Sullivan isn't like those men," he said quietly. He would have thought that the other boys would catch on to that by the way Simon addressed Todd as a doctor and not by his given name. He appealed to the new boy. "He can help you. He stopped me from dying."

The new boy glanced pitifully at Robbie. Robbie let out a heavy breath and relented. "Alright, but at the first sign of funny business, I'm calling the coppers."

It was a hollow threat. If the police knew they all lived and solicited in the park, they'd end up in prison or the workhouse in no time.

"Where does it hurt?" Todd asked the new boy, gesturing for him to sit down.

Simon and the rest of them sat down as well. As Todd questioned the new boy about what had happened to him and how he was feeling, the rest of them made a quick perimeter around them to keep out prying eyes. Most of the time, the finer people walking through the park didn't see what they didn't want to see, so they were safe. The only people who took any notice of them were the gents who would come back after dark for a bit of trade or the police who could end their lives as they knew it. Very occasionally, some nice lady from the Salvation Army or another charity might bring them food or sermonize at them, but for the most part, the boys were left alone.

There was one man in a tweed jacket, his bowler hat pulled low over his eyes, leaning against a tree across the way and watching them, but he didn't seem interested in doing more than watching. Simon had learned to tell when a man wanted to do business and when they were just curious. The tweed man bore watching, but he didn't feel like a customer.

"We all thought you were dead," Robbie confided in Simon as Todd held a hand to the new boy's head, touched his stomach—Simon tried not to be jealous—then opened his suitcase to take out the nearly-empty bottle of aspirin he'd managed to pack before they were kicked out of the boarding house. "We thought that whoever's been doing our sort in got you too."

"Have there been more?" Simon's eyes popped wide.

"They found Bertie dead in the bushes last week," Oliver confirmed in a haunted voice. "And Dick was fished out of a rubbish heap just over on the fancy side of Green Park three days later."

"Strangled, they both were," Robbie whispered. "After being beaten and fucked."

Cold, sad dread pooled in Simon's stomach, and he reached for his own throat. He'd known full well he wasn't the only one to land in hot water. Those sorts of things happened. It was a harsh reminder of how close he'd come to death.

Todd snapped his head up from where he appeared to have just finished treating the new boy, horror in his face. "Strangled?" he asked.

Robbie nodded, though he still radiated hostility at Todd. "What do you care?"

Todd flashed a look at Simon. For some reason, the look made Simon feel guilty, even though getting himself beat up and strangled wasn't his fault.

Simon was on the verge of admitting to Robbie that he might very well have been a target for whoever had killed the other boys when a rustling in the bushes stopped him. A moment later, two more boys—both of whom were in a sorry state—crawled out into the open.

"Are...are you a doctor?" one of them whispered as he glanced at Todd with huge, round eyes.

"I am," Todd told the two in the same sort of angelic voice he'd used when Simon had nearly died. Again, Simon had to fight a wave of jealousy. Todd was his angel. But then, the boys were so obviously hurt, and Todd could help them.

The boy who hadn't spoken burst into tears. The other one said, "My brother was hurt bad. Can you save him?"

Todd gestured for the boys to come all the way out into the patch of shade without hesitating. He set to work asking the same sort of questions he'd had for the new boy, then examining both brothers. Simon rushed to help when he was asked, fishing through the things they'd packed so hastily while fleeing the boarding house to find whatever Todd needed—alcohol, bandages, and the few medicines Todd had.

As soon as the brothers had been treated, another park boy approached them warily, cradling his arm as he did. Once Todd treated him, another showed up, begging for something to stop a deep cut from bleeding. From there, word must have spread through the park that a doctor was there to treat the boys, and that he wasn't asking questions or demanding payment. Simon did what he could to help, but all too soon, he could see that Todd was becoming overwhelmed, not to mention running out of supplies.

"Here."

Simon nearly jumped out of his skin as the man in tweed who had been watching them earlier stepped right up to the group, holding out a box. Several of the boys who were lingering nearby, waiting for Todd to help them, took off at a run. Todd himself was startled by the man.

"As soon as I figured out what you were doing, I popped across the way and bought up everything I could afford," the man in tweed said, setting the box in the grass beside Todd when no one took it from him.

The box was filled with clean bandages, bottles of alcohol, iodine, aspirin, and several medical things that Simon couldn't identify. Todd's eyes went wide with surprise and gratitude.

"Thank you, sir," Todd said, reaching into the box to take out one of the medicine bottles. He glanced across to the edge of the patch of shade, where one of the boys he'd treated earlier sat, and called out, "You, Davy? That was your name. Come back and have one of these pills. It will take the pain away." As soon as Davy came and got his pill, Todd turned to the man in tweed and asked, "Who are you?"

The man touched the brim of his hat and said, "Marcus Albright. I'm a reporter for *The Times*."

A reporter. Simon was both thrilled and wary. Reporters lurked around the park now and then. Sometimes they tried to lure the boys into talking, but most of the time that was only an effort to get names out of them. The papers loved to print stories of the high and mighty misbehaving. They loved to bring men down for hiring out rent-boys. But they never truly helped the boys, especially when they discovered that the boys rarely knew who was paying them for a swallow or a fuck. Simon didn't want to hope that Mr. Albright was different only to be disappointed, but he had bought medical supplies for Todd.

"Thank you for your generosity, Mr. Albright," Todd said as he gestured for one of the boys he hadn't treated yet to come forward. "It is greatly appreciated."

As he set to work examining the boy's cracked lips and miserable teeth, Mr. Albright glanced casually to Robbie. "So what's this about rent-boys from the park turning up dead?"

"You were listening to me," Robbie snapped accusingly, glaring at Mr. Albright.

"How many others have been killed? What did you say their names were? Bertie and what was the other one?"

Simon's shoulder sagged in disappointment as he did his best to assist the boy with the bad teeth. Mr. Albright was just like the others, only interested in a story.

"Fuck off," Robbie sneered at the man. Simon kept his expression neutral, but he shared the man's opinion.

"Don't you want to see the killer captured?" Mr. Albright

asked. "Tell me what you know, and I can help make it happen."

"Are you a detective as well as a reporter?" Oliver snapped at him.

"No," Mr. Albright answered honestly, "but you'd be surprised what the press can do when the police aren't interested."

That statement hit home. The police were only interested in sending boys like them to the workhouse or prison. Maybe a reporter could do something.

No one gave Mr. Albright anymore information, and as time ticked on, everyone, including Mr. Albright, seemed more interested in watching Todd do his work. The afternoon quickly turned into evening, and even the supplies Mr. Albright had purchased ran out.

"I'm sorry, boys," Todd said at last with a sigh. "That's all I can do for today. But I'll try to find a way to help you all again tomorrow."

"You're alright," Robbie said, still frowning, as the young men began to disburse, likely to take up their usual spots for the night. Somehow, Robbie had found a couple of meat pies, and he thrust them out to Simon and Todd before turning and walking off.

Simon didn't realize how hungry he was until he took his first bite of pie. He nearly groaned with how good it was.

"Well, I need to get home and have my supper too," Mr. Albright—who had stayed nearby all afternoon, watching Todd and scribbling on a small notepad—said, touching the brim of his hat. "You know, a doctor who treats the unfortunates in the park would also make a good story, even if it's not the capture of a murderer. Tell me where you live, and I'll come by for a longer interview tomorrow."

Todd glanced up at the man from where he'd moved to sit

by Simon's side in the grass, his meat pie in hand, and laughed wryly. "I'll let you know," he told Mr. Albright.

Simon hid his smile. It was clear that Mr. Albright thought Todd was saying he'd let him know about the story and about where he lived, not that Todd would let him know where he lived once he had a place again.

"We'll be in touch," Mr. Albright said before walking back to the path and heading on his way.

Simon was cautiously grateful for all the reporter had done for them that day, but he was glad once Mr. Albright, and the other boys, had left him and Todd alone. He scooted closer to Todd so that he could finish his pie and smiled at him. When Todd smiled back, Simon thought his heart might burst. As mad as the day had been, it might have been the best day of his life.

Five

Todd was exhausted from work, disturbed by the number of young men he'd treated that afternoon and the nature of their injuries, and anxious about where he and Simon would sleep that night and where they would go in the morning. At the same time, he'd never had a day so filled with purpose as the one he'd just spent.

"I think these boys here in the park need me," he said quietly to Simon once they'd finished their pies and were merely sitting side by side, their arms touching, watching the shadows of evening stretch across the green lawns of Hyde Park. "I doubt any of them have seen any sort of decent medical treatment or care in years."

"In their lives," Simon added in a small, forlorn voice.

Todd glanced to him, his heart aching in his chest. He reached out and took Simon's hand, even though the gesture could be dangerous, if anyone happened to look in their direction. "How did you end up here, Simon?" he asked, already dreading the answer.

Simon shrugged and bit his lip. "Same as any other boy," he murmured. "Ma didn't want me. The orphanage didn't care. Living rough is better than the workhouse, and there's good money to be made, if you have the stomach for it."

"And if you don't end up dead," Todd sighed. He glanced out at the calm waters of the Serpentine, thinking about what Robbie and Albright had both implied earlier—that someone was killing the rent-boys from the park. And as likely as not, no one would care.

It was a painful thought, one Todd didn't want to think about. He squeezed Simon's hand tighter. It had only been a bit more than a fortnight, but he didn't know what he would do if anything happened to Simon. He couldn't imagine being without the kind-hearted young man, especially now that his own situation was so uncertain.

"I guess we should find a safe spot in the bushes to call our own for the night," he told Simon with a wry look.

Simon's eyes went wide. "No, you can't do that," he insisted. "You can't sleep rough. It's not right."

As much as it warmed Todd's heart to have Simon think so highly of him, the situation was what it was. "We've nowhere else to go," he pointed out softly.

Simon grew agitated, shifting to face Todd more fully. "What about your family?" he asked, inspiration lighting his eyes. "You said you have family. You must go to them, ask them to take you in. Surely, they wouldn't turn you away."

Todd laughed ironically. "I'm afraid they *would* turn me away," he sighed, his shoulders dropping. "Otherwise, I would have sought their help long before now."

"But why?" Simon asked, more insistent. "They're your flesh and blood. Don't they have a house? Don't they have a room for you?"

Todd writhed at the idea of even asking. "They do have a house. In Clerkenwell. If they haven't been evicted. But I doubt they'd so much as let me cross the threshold."

"Why?" Simon pressed him. "You're wonderful."

In spite of everything, Todd flushed hot under the praise. He reached for Simon's hand again, but once he had it, he sighed. "My father was disgraced, as I told you. He nearly lost everything to lawsuits. He…he wanted me to marry the daughter of an associate of his. The man offered to pay off all of Father's debts if I did. But I couldn't. I refused. I think you know why."

Simon lowered his head, sending Todd the gentlest, most alluring smile Todd had ever seen. It made his breath catch in his lungs and his heart feel as though it might grow to ten times its size.

"They don't know why I refused, of course," he went on, feeling a mountain of old guilt press down on him. "They just saw me as stubborn and ungrateful. I couldn't deceive the young lady into a marriage she would never be happy in, but I had no concrete way to explain that to my father. He turned his back on me as a result."

"You have to go to him anyhow, Todd," he said in a near whisper. "You aren't meant to live rough." The words "Not like me" hung unspoken between them.

It was an entirely new sensation, one Todd never thought he would feel. He couldn't bear the thought of Simon returning to his old life, couldn't bear to see the darling young man suffer one minute more. His family hated him and considered him the worst sort of traitor, but for Simon's sake, to put a roof over his beloved's head for the night, he would lower himself to face his family again.

"Alright," he said, rising and collecting his suitcase. "We'll give it a try. The worst they can say is no."

In fact, the worst they could say was a great deal more than no. They could chase him away with rocks and sticks. They could call the police to have him removed. They could call on some of their rougher neighbors to hurt them or worse. But it was a risk Todd was willing to take for Simon.

The walk to Clerkenwell was a long and exhausting one. The city was still bustling with evening traffic, which impeded their progress, and the distance was vast, all things considered. It felt symbolic to travel through the opulent surroundings of Mayfair and the shops of Oxford Street, past the middle-class, respectable neighborhoods around Fitzrovia, and on to the rougher, grittier neighborhood of Clerkenwell. His family could have fallen farther. Clerkenwell wasn't as horrible as some of the seedier areas of the city, but it wasn't the sort of place Todd felt comfortable walking through after dark.

It was well after dark when he reached his father's front door. He knocked, then waited, his heart pounding in his throat. After a burst of muffled movement from inside the house, the door flew open, revealing Todd's fifteen-year-old sister, Molly.

"Oh," Molly said, blinking in surprise at the sight of Todd and Simon. "It's you."

"No solicitation," Todd's father's voice sounded from the hall behind Molly. "Whether it's brushes or shoe polish or tickets to the—" He stopped as soon as he spotted Todd on the front step and scowled. "What do you want?" he growled, shoving Molly aside and filling up the doorway in her place.

Todd cleared his throat. "Father," he said, nodding respectfully to the man. "I...the truth is, I've come because I need a place to stay. My associate and I need a place to stay." He turned slightly to gesture to Simon.

Simon's eyes suddenly went wide with surprise, and he took a step back. "I didn't mean..." he started in a whisper. "That is, I didn't think...you don't have to...they're your family."

Todd's heart squeezed. Simon couldn't actually think that he would abandon him, could he? "You are my assistant, Simon," he said, scrambling for a way to communicate to his father that there was nothing untoward about Simon's presence—even though, arguably, there was—and to reassure Simon that he would not be forsaken.

His father narrowed his eyes and glowered at Todd. "And what about that cozy room of yours?" he asked. "What about your position at St. Andrew's?"

Todd cleared his throat and summoned the last scraps of his shredded pride to face his father. "I have no position at St. Andrew's anymore," he confessed. "And I was dismissed from the boarding house. Truly, I have nowhere else to go."

"George, what is the meaning of this commotion?" Todd's mother's voice sounded from inside the house. A moment later, she appeared at his father's side and, exactly like Molly, said, "Oh."

"This one wants our hospitality for the night," Todd's father growled and snorted, as though the notion were ridiculous. "Seems he's gotten himself sacked and thrown out of his room."

For a moment, his mother just stood there, gaping at him. "And you a surgeon," she said at last, shaking her head and clicking her tongue at him in disappointment. "What a waste."

"I will only rely on your hospitality for a short amount of time," Todd said, jaw stiff. He knew asking for his family's help wouldn't go over well. If not for Simon, he would already have walked away. "I am actively seeking a new position, and I expect to be employed again within days."

"Then you'll have yourself another place to rest your traitorous head within days," his father said, starting to shut the door.

"George, wait," Todd's mother said, stopping him. She let out a heavy sigh that sounded more like a hiss, then shook her head again. "He's our son. Whatever betrayals he's guilty of, we cannot forget that."

Todd's father looked like he wanted to argue the point, but instead he grumbled wordlessly and opened the door wider. "The only place we have for him is in the attic," he said.

"The attic will be fine," Todd said, surprised by the relief he felt. If his memory served, the attic had been arranged as a small bedroom for the maid that the family hadn't been able to afford after the first month. It was probably a shambles, but it would do.

His father grumbled more, then stood back, allowing Todd and Simon to enter the house. "This is on you," he told Todd's mother. "I wash my hands of all of it."

He sent Todd one final, disgusted look, then strode off down the hall, disappearing into the family parlor.

Todd's mother looked at him with a combination of disappointment, regret, and irritation. "I trust this will only be for one night. Two or three at the most."

"Yes, Mother," Todd said, trying not to sound as disappointed as he felt as his mother led him and Simon straight up the stairs across the hall from the door. "You'll be rid of me soon enough."

The attic was in as miserable a shape as Todd supposed it would be. Most of it was stuffed with dusty, old boxes and broken bits of furniture. A thin mattress lay on the floor near the space's single window, which was tightly shut. Some sort of vermin had eaten through the bottom corner of the mattress, and for all Todd knew, it could still be inside of the thing.

"You could be living in a comfortable, respectable house right now, if you'd married Mary Holt," his mother sniffed. "But since you were too proud to help your poor father, you won't be too proud for this."

"Mother, I—"

"Mary found herself a nice butcher," his mother cut him off. "She's plump and comfortable and has herself a son now."

Todd's mouth dropped open as he debated whether or not to tell his mother that he was happy for Mary, and her current contentment was the exact reason he'd refused to marry the young woman, but there didn't seem to be much point.

"I'll bring you bedsheets and a pillow for that," Todd's mother said, nodding to the mattress. She glanced between Todd and Simon, then shook her head and said, "You'll have to share. This isn't the Savoy."

Todd almost laughed as his mother turned to go. His mother's suggestion that he and Simon share the bed—if it could even be called that—was all the proof he needed that his family had no idea about his natural inclinations. That would work to his and Simon's advantage, though. It was one less reason for his parents to call the police.

While they waited for his mother to return with bedding, Todd set his suitcase down and moved to the window, and Simon set to work tidying up the space they'd been given. It took a bit of banging and shoving, but Todd finally managed to open the window. A few birds that had been standing on the edge of the roof flew off with disgruntled squawks, but the rush of fresh air—or what passed for fresh air in the city—was a blessing.

By the time his mother returned, the attic was already more presentable. Molly entered the attic right behind her, carrying a pitcher of wash water and a rag.

"This is all I could find," his mother said, dropping the bedding on the mattress and gesturing for Molly to put the pitcher and rag down on a small pile of boxes. "You'll have to make due. And I'm not certain that I'll have enough to go around for breakfast in the morning, so you'll have to fend for yourself. Your father doesn't approve of any of this."

She spoke the last words as though they were the only ones that mattered, sniffed, then turned and left, Molly following her. Molly sent a final, wary look at Simon over her shoulder before shutting the attic door with perhaps a little too much force. Todd stood where he was for a moment, listening to the sound of their footsteps retreating down the stairs.

"Well, that went better than I expected," Todd said, his voice thick with irony, once he and Simon were alone.

When he turned, he was surprised to find that Simon wore a smile of contentment. "This will do nicely," Simon said as he looked around.

The lad never failed to amaze and humble him. "It's better than sleeping rough in Hyde Park?" he asked.

"Oh, yes," Simon said, reaching for the bedding. "There's a roof over our head, a soft place for us to sleep, and we'll be able to wash." He nodded to the pitcher as he shook the bedsheet out, then spread it over the horrible mattress.

Todd moved to help him make the bed. "You astound me with your optimism, Simon," he said with a tender smile. A moment later, his face pinched. "I'll find something better for you soon, I promise."

Simon glanced across the bed they were making with genuine surprise. "This is magnificent," he said. "And…and I can't believe that you kept me with you." He lowered his eyes. "You didn't have to. I would have gone."

The shy, meek expression went straight to Todd's heart. "Of course I kept you with me," he said, climbing onto the mattress once they had the bedsheet tucked around it. "I don't think I could bear to be parted from you."

Simon's eyes went wide, and he drew in a breath. For a moment, he merely gaped at Todd. Then he said, "Truly?"

"Truly," Todd repeated.

He wasn't entirely certain what drove him to do it, other

than the call of his heart, but he reached for Simon, drawing him onto the bed and into his arms. Their kiss that morning had been interrupted, and there was a fair chance that anything they did now could be interrupted as well, but it was worth the risk. Still feeling woefully uncertain about how to go about things, he cupped a hand behind Simon's head and leaned in to touch his lips to Simon's. Simon practically purred in response and shuffled closer to Todd, sliding his arms around him. He deepened their kiss, as though tutoring Todd in the ways of love, but as soon as Todd found the courage to take the lead, Simon conceded everything to him.

It was beautiful and perfect, and once he started, Todd couldn't stop. He shifted his hands to hold the sides of Simon's face for a moment as he kissed him with all of the affection that swirled within him, then moved his hands restlessly over Simon's body. He wanted to touch him, embrace him, learn everything about him, but he had no idea where to start or what to do. Simon seemed to know what he wanted more than he did.

Simon swiftly undid the buttons of Todd's jacket and pushed it off his shoulders. He went straight to work on the rest of Todd's buttons after that, working through them with deft fingers. Todd reciprocated, but his hands were so unsteady on the fastenings of Simon's clothes that he laughed at himself for making a mess of things.

"I don't know what I'm doing," he confessed as he shrugged out of his jacket and waistcoat while Simon tugged the hem of his shirt out of his trousers.

"It's not difficult," Simon whispered, helping Todd sweep his shirt up over his head.

Once Todd was naked from the waist up, Simon's eyes filled with heat and want. He spread his hands over Todd's chest, burrowing his slender fingers through the hair there. Nothing had ever felt so sensual in Todd's life. He wasn't prepared for the overwhelming lust and love Simon's touch inspired in him, and he was even less prepared for the way his body and soul sang when Simon glanced up into his eyes with a look of perfect adoration.

It was so endearing that Todd took Simon's face in his hands again and kissed him as though he had been kissing him his whole life. Kissing Simon was the easiest thing in the world, and while everything else was still a mystery, he committed himself to solving that mystery in every way possible.

Somehow, they shed the rest of their clothes and shoes, then stretched out on the bed.

"I want to give you everything," Todd whispered between kisses, bristling with desperate energy, "but I don't know how."

"I can show you," Simon insisted, nudging Todd to his back. "Please let me show you."

Todd didn't know what to say. He could barely form thoughts as Simon nudged his legs apart and settled between them. He couldn't remember what thoughts were as Simon leaned in to kiss him—first his lips, then his stubbly cheek, then the line of his neck. Todd couldn't contain his sounds of pleasure as Simon kissed his way down to his chest, even though he knew what Simon was doing was barely skimming the surface of everything that could be done. He was so intoxicated by the lines and planes of Simon's body, the way he looked, and the way his warm skin felt in his hands. He'd seen all of Simon before while treating his injuries, but this was something entirely new and different.

Simon didn't stop at kissing his chest and licking his nipples. He continued down across the flat of Todd's stomach, veering to the side to brush his lips across Todd's hip. Todd knew what was going to happen, but he was still shocked into a deep groan when Simon stroked a hand up his hot, hard cock and brought his mouth down to tease the tip. It felt so amazing that Todd nearly bucked off the mattress. The way Simon worked his hand up and down Todd's shaft while licking off the moisture that had formed on his tip and drawing it into his mouth was beyond too much. Before Todd was halfway aware of his body's reactions, he came hard, spurting across Simon's lips and chin.

He should have been mortified, but the sight of Simon looking downright impish with Todd's essence splashed across his sensual lips was the most erotic thing Todd had ever seen. And when Simon's pink tongue darted out to lick his lips, as though they were covered with honey and not semen, if Todd could have come a second time, he would have.

"I'm sorry," he panted as Simon daintily wiped his face and slid his body across Todd's until they were face to face again. "I'm so sorry. That was too soon. I should have lasted longer."

Simon shook his head, utterly confident as he gazed down at Todd. "You're not used to it," he said. "But you will be in time."

Todd caught his breath at that statement. It implied a future. It implied not just one additional encounter at some point, but many.

"What about you?" he asked, stroking the side of Simon's face and threading his fingers through Simon's hair. "Are you…satisfied."

Simon's eyes went wider. "Do you want me to be?"

"Yes, love, of course," Todd murmured. He pushed himself up to capture Simon's mouth with his. After kissing him until he was breathless, he rested back against the pillow, then said, "I always want you to be just as satisfied as I am. I'm just not certain how…." He was too embarrassed to admit he didn't know how to make Simon feel as good as Simon had made him feel.

Simon's pink lips spread into the most coquettish smile Todd had ever seen, making him wish he weren't already spent. He reached for Todd's hand and drew it between their two bodies, coaxing Todd to caress his cock. Simon was already hard and made the most beautiful sounds as he guided Todd in the right way to stroke him. Once Todd had the way of it, he stroked Simon lavishly on his own.

"If we had the slippery stuff with us, I'd want you to fuck me," Simon moaned, moving his hips restlessly to make the most of the way Todd stroked him. "I want to feel you stretch and breech me," he went on, his eyes fluttering shut and his expression hinting that he was imagining everything he said. "I want to feel you inside of me, to know that I am yours completely."

"Yes," Todd gasped, his cock twitching as though it liked the idea. "Yes, I want that too." He'd never imagined he'd ever do something like that, but the idea of possessing Simon and giving them both pleasure as he did consumed him now.

"I just want to be yours," Simon purred, moving faster against Todd's hand. "Yours, yours, forever and only yours. Oh!"

A burst of liquid warmth spread across Todd's hand and belly. He'd never experienced another man coming before, and marveled at the tension and release in Simon's body, the sounds he made, and the way he lost all energy and collapsed atop him once he was done. It was the most beautiful thing Todd had ever been a part of in his life. He shifted so that he could wrap his arms around Simon and press his lips to the side of Simon's head as it rested against his shoulder. The two of them were overheated and sticky, the attic was dirty and shabby, but Todd had never been happier in his life.

And even though the rest of his life was a sea of endless uncertainty stretching out in all directions, he knew one thing for certain. Come what may, he would never let Simon go.

Six

Simon had never known the sort of contentment that he awoke with the next morning. His life was nothing but uncertainty, his surroundings were shabby and tenuous, and his stomach growled with hunger that he wasn't sure when he'd be able to satisfy, but he was naked and in bed with Todd. Nothing else mattered. He stretched in contentment, reveling in the way his skin felt against Todd's. Todd was bigger than him, but not by much. Their bodies fit together perfectly, and as soon as he could beg, borrow, or steal a bit of the slippery stuff, he longed for their bodies to be as one.

That thought had his morning wood twitching into even greater hardness. Simon allowed himself one glorious moment to enjoy it and to entertain the thought of waking Todd up by sucking him off. There were too many sounds coming from the house below, though. It was far, far too great a risk for him and Todd to be caught together that way, especially when Simon was fully aware that Todd's family was absolutely Todd's last resort.

Instead, he lifted himself up enough to beam down at his

angel's sleeping face, then threw caution to the wind and lowered himself to kiss Todd's lips. Like some sort of fairy story, Todd drew in a breath and woke up. He stretched and groaned, filling Simon with every delicious sensation and emotion he'd ever known. Damn anyone who told him a fortnight wasn't enough time to fall completely in love with someone. He loved Todd with everything he had, everything he ever would have, and no one could tell him otherwise.

Todd's eyes fluttered open, and he broke into a smile at the sight of Simon above him. "Good morning," he mumbled.

"Good morning, my angel," Simon whispered back. He was too afraid that the perfect moment would vanish if he did more than whisper.

A bright sort of surprise filled Todd's eyes, and he shifted so that he could pull Simon atop him. Simon shivered as Todd ran his hands up and down his back, cupping his arse for far too short a moment, then muscled himself up to kiss Simon's lips. Simon indulged in the kiss for only a second before flinching away.

"No," he murmured. "My breath is terrible. And your family is awake."

Todd growled in his throat in a way that had Simon shivering. "I don't care about your breath, I just like kissing you."

The sentiment was so beautiful that Simon nearly burst into tears. "Still," he said, reluctantly pulling away from Todd and rolling to crouch beside the mattress, "we should get up and dress so that we can be gone as quickly as possible."

He stood, not realizing until after he'd already done it that he'd stepped into a sunbeam from the attic's single window. Todd sucked in a breath as he gazed at Simon's naked body, heat and need filling his eyes. It felt scintillating and wonderful to have Todd look at him that way—so much so that he was tempted to stretch and preen and give his angel everything to look at and more.

A clatter of someone dropping something near the bottom of the stairs on the other side of the attic door reminded him of just how precarious their position was. Instead of making a spectacle of himself for Todd, Simon jumped over to the boxes where the pitcher of wash water stood and set to work bathing.

Todd rose from the mattress and joined him. He stepped right up behind Simon, grasping Simon's arms and pressing his front along the full length of Simon's back. That included grinding his half-erect cock against the cleft of Simon's backside. Simon shuddered and let out a whimper of desire as he leaned into Todd.

"I want it too," Todd whispered in his ear, moving his hands down to grip Simon's hips so that he could arch against him even more definitively. "I don't know how to do it, but I want it. As soon as we can, I want you to show me how."

They were the most magical words anyone had ever said to Simon. "Yes," he breathed out, closing his eyes. Everything within him ached and pulsed to give himself over to Todd completely. He wanted Todd to use him in every way he'd ever been used, even the ones he hadn't liked with other men. With Todd, it would all mean something different, something beautiful and special for just the two of them.

"Molly!" a shout sounded from the hallway downstairs. "Get away from there. I will not have you coddling your brother in any way."

Todd leapt back from Simon just in time to hear footsteps dashing down one or two stairs, then running along the hall. Simon prickled with anxiety, and he wondered how close he and Todd had come to disaster. The attic door was still firmly shut, thank God.

Todd cleared his throat and set about gathering the clothes they'd shed the night before and fetching moderately clean ones from the suitcase. "We need to be more careful," he said, his voice gruff.

"Yes." It was the only thing Simon could think to say.

They rushed through morning ablutions, both of them aware of how important it was for them to be fully dressed and seemingly impartial to each other. They took special care to remake the bed and to examine it to be certain there were no lingering stains, in case anyone thought to investigate. The trouble was that they had made a bit of a mess. Simon could only hope no one bothered to check the sheets before he and Todd could be on their way.

They were close to ready to descend from the attic when Todd stuck his hand in his jacket pocket and pulled out a business card. He frowned at it.

"What is that?" Simon asked.

Todd continued to frown as he studied the card. "It was given to me yesterday by a man named Lionel Mercer when I inquired about a position at a chemist."

Todd and Simon walked to the door and finally descended from the attic. Todd seemed to know his way around the house, so Simon followed him.

"This Mercer fellow seemed to think he could find me a position at a hospital," Todd went on.

"Even though the hospitals refused to see you?" Simon asked.

Todd flinched and turned to him in surprise. "How did you know that?"

Simon shrugged bashfully. "You've said enough things for me to guess. And if they weren't turning you away, you'd have a position already, because you're wonderful."

Todd smiled gratefully at him, then continued down to the ground floor. "At this point, I don't think I have much choice other than to visit the law offices of Dandie & Wirth."

"Is that where you're going today, then?" Simon asked.

"Yes," Todd said as they headed down the back hall toward what smelled like a kitchen. "Would you like to come with me?"

"Oh, no," Simon protested, his eyes round. "They're solicitors. They're far too grand for me."

"I'm certain they aren't," Todd said. His face pinched before he went on with, "But I understand if you'd rather stay behind. Or perhaps return to the park to check on your friends?"

The way Todd said it made Simon feel as though it were a request. Todd was a healer. He probably wanted to know how his patients were faring. Simon nodded at him with a smile.

They'd just stepped into the kitchen, but instead of receiving even a moderately warm welcome—and perhaps some tea and bread—Todd's mother was there to glower at them.

"I said I didn't have any breakfast for you," the woman said, wiping her hands on the apron she wore. "I won't have you two eating me out of house and home."

"I was just on my way out to see about a hospital position," Todd said in a gruff voice, crossing through the kitchen. Simon couldn't tell if he was angry or hurt by his own mother's coldness. Either way, he marched straight to the door, turning back to Simon once he had the door open to say, "I will check back with you later. Stay out of trouble."

Simon smiled and nodded, but he was too overwhelmed with uncertainty as Todd left to say anything. As soon as the door was shut and Todd was gone, his smile vanished. He glanced fearfully to Todd's mother.

The woman narrowed her eyes at him. "You look like you've got a pair of strong arms on you," she said.

Simon didn't, but he knew where the comment was leading. "What do you need me to do?"

Todd's mother sniffed. "Go through the house and empty the chamber pots. When you're done with that, I need someone to scour the pots."

Simon nodded and retreated swiftly back into the house. He wasn't surprised that Todd's mother would give him the lowliest and dirtiest jobs to do. Clearly, the family didn't have a scullery maid. He would do what he needed to do in order to pay for what little room and board he and Todd were given, and he would do it without complaint. He said nothing as he passed both Mr. Sullivan and Molly on the stairs in his search for chamber pots. He could find them himself.

Not only did he empty and wash the chamber pots, then scrub pots in the scullery, within an hour, Todd's mother had him cleaning out the grates in the downstairs fireplaces. At least she'd given him a heel of stale bread and a cup of water for his troubles.

He had his head and shoulders deep inside one of the fireplaces and was covered in soot when there was a knock on the front door and Molly went to answer it.

"Is your father at home?" a deep, growling voice asked.

Simon gasped and nearly cried out in terror. He knew the voice. It was the voice of the Devil. He would never forget that voice as long as he lived.

"I'll fetch him," Molly said blandly, as if she had no idea what sort of evil had just entered her home.

Simon kept his head and shoulders inside of the fireplace, but he turned in an effort to get a look at the visitor. He only caught the barest glimpse, but it was enough. It was him—the man who had lured him into a carriage with the promise of double his usual pay, battered and fucked him, then beat him and strangled him, insisting he'd never live to tell a soul what happened to him, then left him for dead.

"Ah, Keller, what brings you here so early?" Mr. Sullivan greeted the Devil as though they were friends.

They moved out of eyesight, but Simon could still hear when the devil—Keller—said, "I need your medical services, George, if you still remember how to sew people up."

Mr. Sullivan hummed and made a sound of alarm. "What caused this?"

"I was attacked by a dog," Keller said. "The beast scratched my face and bit me several times."

"Those don't look like dog bites," Mr. Sullivan said as their voices retreated farther down the hall.

"It was a dog, I tell you," Keller boomed, furious. "A *dead* dog."

Simon gulped and moved away from the fireplace, dropping the brush he'd been cleaning it with into the bucket of sooty water. He might not have ever been to school or learned to read, but he knew what he was hearing when he heard it. Everything suddenly fit together in his mind. Bertie, Dick, him. This Keller man, whoever he was, was the one going around killing the boys from the park.

Simon didn't hesitate. He bolted for the door, throwing it open and rushing outside. Once in the street, he turned west and broke into a run. He didn't stop running until he was several streets away. Even then, he kept up a fast pace. He had to get to Hyde Park as soon as possible to tell Robbie and Oliver, and maybe even Mr. Albright, if the man was still there, what he knew.

It took him the better part of the morning to travel across London on foot. He must have looked—and possibly smelled —a fright from cleaning fireplaces, because most of the people he passed on the street turned their noses up at him. He was followed by a policeman for a few streets before cutting through a back alley and making a few unexpected turns to lose the man. When he walked past a square with a small fountain in the middle, he paused to scrub away as much of the soot and smell as he could, but one of the residents of the square caught him bathing and chased him away.

He was certain he looked like the wretch that he was by the time he reached Hyde Park and made his way to the far side and the shrubs where his friends had their patch. But instead of being greeted happily by them, he found them all huddled together, eyes wide, looking nearly feral.

"Has something happened?" he asked as he approached them.

Robbie peeled away from the pack, looking like he would attack or pick a fight at first, but gaping when he saw it was Simon. He raked Simon up and down with a look, then nearly smiled as he said, "Have you found work as a chimney sweep, then?"

Simon shook his head. "I was cleaning fireplaces, but a man showed up named Keller who said he was bit by a dog, but he was the man who nearly killed me." It was a clumsy explanation and the words came out in a jumbled rush, but it was all the information Robbie and the others needed to hear.

The boys gaped at Simon as though he were telling a ghost story.

"Davy was found dead this morning," Robbie said in a hushed voice. "Same as the others—beaten, fucked, and strangled."

Simon's gut clenched hard. "It was him. I know it was him. It was Keller."

"Who's Keller?" the new boy from the day before asked. Simon fleetingly noticed that he was looking much better after the treatment Todd had given him.

Simon shook his head and shrugged. "I don't know. Todd's father said that was his name."

"Todd?" Robbie asked, squinting. "Is that your man? Dr. Sullivan?"

Simon nodded vigorously.

Robbie's look darkened. "I knew that doctor was no good. What's a killer doing at his house?"

"It's not Todd's house," Simon burst out, angry at Robbie's assumptions and ready to defend Todd to the death. "It's his family's house, and his family doesn't like him any more than any of ours likes us."

The boys seemed to soften at the hint that Todd wasn't so different from them. They must have remembered how kind Todd had been the day before and how he'd helped them.

"But you say the murderer is at your man's family's house?" Oliver asked.

Simon nodded.

"Where is your man, then?" Robbie asked, looking nervous. "Not with the murderer, I hope?"

Simon's gut clenched tightly and his throat closed up. "He can't go back there," he said hoarsely, though to no one in particular. "He can't go back to that house. Not if the Devil is there."

"Where is he, then?" Oliver asked.

"He…he went to see about a job. He went to—" His face pinched as he tried to remember where. "He went to a place called Dandie & Wirth."

The boys all blinked and glanced around at each other. None of them seemed to have a clue what Simon was talking about.

"I think it's a law office," Simon added.

"The coppers?" one of the boys standing at the back of the group said, then dashed away, as if the police were on the way and he needed to hide.

"Sounds hoity-toity," Robbie said.

"I need to find him," Simon gulped, taking a few steps

away from the group. "I need to find Dandie & Wirth and tell Todd that he can't go back to Clerkenwell. I need to tell him Keller is the Devil."

He started away from Robbie, Oliver, and the others at a jog, but before he reached the end of the Serpentine, he stopped and doubled over, panting as he rested his hands against his knees. He didn't have the first idea where Dandie & Wirth was, which meant he didn't know where Todd was. He straightened and stared around at the tall buildings ringing the park, pulse pounding with desperation. The man who had tried to kill him was on the loose, he'd killed another boy, and Todd was lost somewhere in London, far away from him.

Seven

The Law Office of Dandie & Wirth was located at the edge of The City, in a nondescript building that was home to several discreet businesses. Each of the doors off the ground floor hallway was marked with little more than a brass plaque that announced the name of the business without giving much description about what it was. It was enough to make Todd wonder what sort of secretive world he'd wandered into. Calling on Mr. Lionel Mercer had seemed like a good idea—the only idea he had—when he set out from Clerkenwell first thing in the morning, but as he stood in front of the plain door, he had his doubts.

He knocked anyhow, and was greeted by a muffled call of, "Come in," in a voice he recognized as Mercer's.

As soon as Todd turned the handle and opened the door into the small, cozy office, his worries vanished. He wasn't certain why, but he knew he'd sought help in the right place. The office had been decorated by someone with an artistic eye. Bookshelves lined the front room that contained the standard reading fare, but also a plethora of curiosities and exotic art pieces that Todd found attractive…and vaguely arousing. A pair of leather upholstered sofas stood facing each other in the center of the room on an expensive-looking oriental carpet, and a stove containing a cheerfully-steaming kettle took up one corner. Taken as a whole, Todd felt as though he'd been invited to tea rather than calling on a solicitor.

"Ah, Dr. Sullivan, we meet again," Mercer said, stepping out from behind a dazzling, mahogany desk. The desk was arranged opposite the door and perfectly placed between two windows in such a way that it drew the eye. Judging by the somewhat posed position Mercer was in when Todd walked through the door—the light from the windows hitting him just right and infusing his porcelain-perfect skin with warmth—Todd assumed the point was to draw the eye straight to Mercer. Mercer was easily the most intimidatingly beautiful man Todd had ever seen, with his pale skin, piercing blue eyes, and regal mannerisms.

"I wasn't certain where else to go," Todd told him, shuffling in his spot as if he didn't know whether he should remove his coat and hat, lounge on the sofas, or remain formal.

"Not to worry," Mercer said, sweeping up to him so that he could remove Todd's hat and coat for him. "You're in good hands now. Hands that take care of their own."

"I beg your pardon?" Todd asked, twisting awkwardly as Mercer tugged his coat from his shoulders, then carried it and his hat to a stand near the door. Todd's feeling from the day before that Mercer recognized him as a kindred sort of man returned.

"I have an eye for these things," Mercer explained, though what he was explaining was a mystery to Todd. "And I asked around."

"You…asked around?" Todd's nerves bristled. "About me?"

"Yes," Mercer said, crossing to the stove and pouring a cup of tea. "Though I must admit, it was difficult to obtain the proper information about you. It seems you keep mostly to yourself, Dr. Todd Sullivan, but I was able to discover what I needed to in the end."

"It's been less than twenty-four hours," Todd said in an overwhelmed voice.

"I am very good at what I do." Mercer glanced over his shoulder at Todd with a look that was as impish as it was flirtatious.

Todd was at a complete loss for what to say. Fortunately, he was spared embarrassment when a second man—a tall man with dark hair and a handsome but shrewd face—stepped into the room. He read a file of some sort as he walked and, without looking up from it at first, said, "Don't frighten the poor man, Lionel. If what you said was true, he's come to us for help."

Todd could only gape, feeling even more out of his depth, as the dark-haired man closed the file and set it on the desk, then crossed the room to him and held out a hand.

"David Wirth," he introduced himself. "Solicitor and solver of problems for the members of the Brotherhood."

"I beg your pardon," Todd asked, blinking rapidly. "The Brotherhood?" Belatedly, he remembered his manners and shook Mr. Wirth's hand.

Wirth tilted his head and studied Todd for a moment. "You're not a member of the Brotherhood?"

"Not yet," Mercer answered for Todd, bringing him a cup of tea, then moving to stand by Wirth's side. "We'll fix that soon enough, though. At present, Dr. Sullivan is a lost and wandering soul in desperate need of both the camaraderie of the Brotherhood and my personal help."

Wirth grinned at Mercer in such a way that left Todd wondering whether the two were lovers. But no, that was impossible. There might not have been anyone else in the office, but it was still considered a public place. Surely, the two men wouldn't risk showing affection to each other when a strange man who could report them to the police was with them.

"I have never heard of the Brotherhood," Todd said, glancing between the two men.

"Of course you haven't," Mercer said with a glint in his eyes. "Secrecy is a necessity with an organization such as ours."

"It is a social organization, of sorts, for men like us," Wirth explained.

Todd blinked at him. "I'm sorry?"

"Inverts," Mercer said, looking as though he might laugh. "Uranians. Sodomites. I believe the Germans are now using the term 'homosexuals'."

All of the blood felt as though it drained from Todd's face, and his hands and feet instantly went numb with panic. "I don't…there must be…I never said…."

"Don't worry," Wirth reassured him, the picture of calm. "This is a safe place for the Brotherhood. One of many. We'll get you enrolled in our numbers as soon as possible. We have a club on Park Lane, The Chameleon Club, where members meet for social occasions and the like. As I said, we help each other out in a variety of ways, providing everything from free meals to excuses as to why someone chooses not to marry—"

"Or understanding ladies of a similar nature if they simply must," Mercer interrupted.

"—to legal aid," Wirth finished, sending Mercer a scolding look for the interruption. He gestured to the office in general.

"And positions with trusted employers," Mercer added, stepping back to the stand where he'd deposited Todd's coat and hat just moments ago to retrieve them. "Which is where our business lies."

"Unlike so many clubs in London," Wirth explained as Mercer returned to Todd to hand him his coat and hat while simultaneously taking away the tea that Todd had been too stunned to so much as look at, "the Brotherhood does not limit their membership based on class or income. Yes, we have titled gentlemen in our ranks—"

"Two dukes among them," Mercer added from the stove.

"—but we have just as many tradesmen and gentlemen in our organization as well," Wirth finished, barely acknowledging Mercer's interruption. "The Chameleon Club offers a small number of rooms to members who have run up against hard times, but the greater focus is on helping men to lead productive and satisfying lives of independence, without interference from the law or society."

It wasn't so much the words Wirth used to describe the purpose of the Brotherhood as the significant looks he sent Todd as he spoke that had Todd's jaw dropping to the floor and his heart soaring with hope and gratitude for men like them. Perhaps there was kindness and optimism in the world after all.

"I don't know what to say," he said, glancing from Wirth to Mercer.

"Say nothing for now," Mercer said, plucking Todd's coat from his arm and moving to help him put it on. "We have a call to pay at London Hospital."

"London Hospital?" Todd was stunned.

When Mercer moved around to Todd's front to button his coat for him, he had a mischievous gleam in his blue eyes. Todd was too overwhelmed to do anything about it or to question the man. He could only follow as Mercer fetched his own coat and hat, then led Todd back out into the bustling city.

"I think you will find that one of the benefits of the Brotherhood," Mercer explained as they walked, "is that its members have connections in every field and every discipline. We will have you employed as a surgeon by lunchtime, I am certain."

"I would be eternally grateful," Todd said. His head spun with the turn of events he'd experienced.

But when they reached London Hospital and made their way into its offices to speak with one of the administrators—a feat that Todd considered a miracle in and of itself—they were given an answer that Mercer clearly hadn't anticipated.

"We are not hiring at present, Mr. Mercer," the administrator said. He glanced to Todd with a somewhat guilty frown. "Your friend will have to look elsewhere."

Todd wasn't at all surprised by the curtness of the dismissal. He'd already inquired at London Hospital, and the answer had been the same. Mercer seemed shocked, though.

"I've never had anything quite so puzzling happen in my life," Mercer said as he and Todd walked away from the august hospital in defeat. "It is almost inconceivable."

Todd was tempted to laugh, but he didn't want to offend Mercer. "It is precisely what I expected," he sighed. "For more than a fortnight now, that is the sort of answer I have received to inquiries for employment at every hospital I've tried."

"And which hospitals have you tried?" Mercer asked, pausing at the street corner, ignoring the traffic around them.

Todd gave the man a list of all the places he'd been. Mercer's eyes grew wide at the length of the list. He nodded as Todd finished, seeming to come to a decision about something.

"Is your heart set on working at one of the larger institutions, or might you be interested in employment at a smaller hospital, perhaps in the east end, that caters to charity cases?" Mercer asked he walked on.

Todd shrugged and followed. "I would be willing to take any position that allows me to heal the sick."

Mercer hummed in approval, and they walked on. They caught an omnibus that took them across town, all the way into Poplar, to a hospital Todd had yet to inquire at. It was small and teeming with patients who wouldn't possibly be able to pay for their treatment. As pitiful as the sight was, it gave Todd hope. The hospital was obviously understaffed and needed him.

But when Mercer managed to get them in to see the head doctor, Todd's hopes were dashed.

"Sullivan, you say?" the doctor asked, eyeing Todd suspiciously. "Dr. Todd Sullivan?"

"Yes, that is his name," Mercer said, his puzzled frown hinting that he, too sensed things weren't as they should be.

The doctor took one last, regret-filled look at Todd then said, "No, I'm sorry. We don't have the funding to take on a surgeon at the moment. You'll have to go."

The dismissal meant that Todd was not—as Mercer had promised—employed by lunchtime.

"Something is decidedly odd about this entire thing," Mercer said, almost as though he were talking to himself, as he and Todd made their way back to the omnibus stop. "I've never known a charity hospital to turn away a qualified surgeon without so much as interviewing him. And the man seemed to know your name."

"I have a very bad feeling I know why," Todd sighed.

His hunch was proven correct an hour later, when he and Mercer called at another small hospital—one that was, ironically, close to his family's home in Clerkenwell.

"Todd Sullivan?" the head nurse who they'd been allowed to speak with at that hospital said, looking down her nose at

Todd. She shook her head. "No, we've been warned against him."

"You've been—I beg your pardon?" Mercer asked, blinking in offense.

The nurse shrugged. "Dr. Keller has put the word out about Dr. Sullivan. He says that any hospital that hires the man will lose patrons, be plagued with accidents, and have the police called on them."

"For what infractions?" Mercer asked, indignant.

The nurse shook her head. "I don't know, and I don't want to find out."

Five minutes later, Todd and Mercer were back on the street.

"Keller is the one who dismissed me from St. Andrew's," Todd explained with a sigh.

"And you said it was all because you treated a rent-boy on his deathbed whom you had found in the alley beside the hospital?" Mercer asked. Todd had given him more details about finding Simon during their journey through the city, and when he nodded, Mercer tapped his chin and said, "This is all decidedly odd."

"I need to check on that boy," Todd said, his heart squeezing with concern for Simon. "That man," he corrected himself. "I left him with my parents at a house near here this morning. I—I'm deeply concerned for his welfare." Considering everything Todd had learned about the Brotherhood and Mercer's nature since that morning, he was reasonably certain Mercer would understand the implications about his relationship with Simon.

"I'll accompany you," Mercer said, surprising Todd. "And then we'll see if we cannot untie the Gordian knot your Dr. Keller has bound you with."

But ten minutes later, when they reached the Sullivan

house, Todd's anxieties doubled when his mother met him at the door and thrust his packed suitcase at him.

"One night was more than enough," she said, making a shooing gesture once Todd had his suitcase. "You're no longer wanted here."

"Where is Simon?" Todd asked, his heart slamming against his ribs with sudden panic.

His father appeared in the doorway, then advanced, pushing Todd and Mercer back several feet onto the street. "Who knows what became of that little blighter. He ran off in a hurry as soon as Keller arrived."

"Keller?" Todd's brow flew up in alarm, and his pulse raced so hard he thought he might be sick. "What was he doing here?"

"What business is it of yours if an old friend calls on me?" his father growled. "Keller was the one who told me about boys like your so-called assistant latching onto imbeciles like you and bleeding them dry. If I find that so much as a farthing has been pilfered from this house, I'll hold you responsible."

"Simon is no thief," Todd hissed. He wasn't inclined to battle with his father, though. All he wanted to do was find Simon and make certain his love was safe.

"We'll see about that," his father sniffed, then unceremoniously marched back into the house and slammed the door behind him.

A moment of brittle silence filled the air before Mercer said, "What a charming family you have."

The gentle quip was enough to break the tension gripping Todd and he laughed, but only for a moment. After that, his face fell. "We have to find Simon," he said. "Something isn't right here, and I cannot help but feel Simon is in danger."

Eight

"Excuse me, sir, but do you know where I can find Dandie & Wirth?" Simon asked a well-dressed gentleman strolling through the busiest part of Hyde Park, a handsomely-dressed lady who must have been his wife on his arm.

The gentleman turned up his nose at Simon and hurried on, whisking his wife away with him and saying, "Mind your pockets, Maude. The wretch was probably trying to pick them."

Simon let out a breath in despair and hurried away. He'd been asking about Dandie & Wirth for hours. At best, the people he'd asked hadn't had any idea what he was talking about. At worst, they'd attempted to call the coppers on him. One older lady had beat him with her closed parasol, which had caused a scene. Simon had been forced to run to the other side of the park and hide in the bushes for several minutes after that.

He wasn't going to give up, though. He had to find Todd, had to warn him about Keller. It was likely too late to catch his angel at Dandie & Wirth's, since hours had passed, but perhaps the man who had given Todd his card would know where Todd had gone.

"Pardon me, miss, but do you know where Dandie & Wirth's office is?" he approached a young woman pushing a pram, probably a nanny.

"Stay away from the child," the woman growled at him, as though the baby in the pram were made of diamonds and Simon were intent on stealing it.

Simon hurried off in the opposite direction, despondent. It wasn't that he believed Todd would abandon him, especially not after the night they'd just had. Simon didn't know how to find his angel again, though. Panic gripped him over the idea that he and Todd could end up lost to each other. It was part of the reason he'd been unwilling to leave Hyde Park until he knew with absolute certainty where Dandie & Wirth's was. Todd would look for him in the park if all else failed, but Hyde Park was enormous.

"Excuse me, sir," he tried yet again, though his voice had grown hoarse from asking, and his heart wasn't in it in the same way it had been at first. "Do you happen to know where I could find the office of Dandie & Wirth?" He went so far as to tug on the sleeve of the man who was walking briskly along the path that would lead to the Serpentine.

The man turned and fixed Simon with a dark scowl. A second later, both Simon and the man gasped and flinched as they recognized each other. Simon had unwittingly tugged on the sleeve of the Devil.

"You!" the Devil—Keller, if the way Todd's father had addressed the man was right—snapped.

"No!" Simon backpedaled, desperate to get away from the man. "No, not you. Leave me alone!" His panic made him clumsy, and as he tried to get away, he tripped over his own feet and tumbled to the gravel of the path.

Keller wore a look of fury mingled with alarm as he

twisted this way and that, glancing around at the people nearby. Simon wasn't certain what the man was doing at first. He wouldn't have cared and would have thought of nothing but scrambling to get away from Keller, but as soon as Keller was satisfied about whatever he'd looked around for, he lunged toward Simon, grabbing Simon's threadbare jacket with both hands and wrenching him to his feet.

"Do you know who I am?" Keller growled, holding his face so close to Simon's that the heat of his breath warmed Simon's face.

Simon nodded in terror, eyes wide and mouth half open in a silent scream that he couldn't get out. He remembered the way Keller had picked him out of the lads who were cruising for custom on that night over a fortnight ago. He remembered the feeling that it wasn't going to be a good night, the way Keller had shoved him into a dark carriage, even though he didn't want to go. He remembered the way the man had forced his mouth open and choked him with his prick, then shoved him around so that he could breech him. He remembered telling himself it would all be over soon, then he'd be able to afford a bowl of soup and some bread, that it would be worth it. Then he remembered the kicks and the blows, the hands around his neck, and the world going dark as Keller growled at him that he'd never tell a soul what had happened.

Keller had been wrong. Simon had told a soul. He just hadn't known the Devil's name. Until now. Now he could tell.

"Let me go," he wailed, thrashing and kicking to get away from Keller. "Let me go!"

Simon had never regretted being slight of build with underdeveloped muscles before. He knew it had served him well in his business in the park. But as Keller hissed, "Shut up!" at him and dragged him off the path and toward a thick clump of shrubs, he prayed that he would miraculously have the strength and the heft to fight Keller off. His life depended on it.

"You and I have unfinished business," Keller growled, pushing and shoving and manhandling Simon toward the bushes. "I should have made certain I finished it that night."

Simon shouted wordlessly, but rather than rush to help, the few people walking in that part of the park who saw what was happening turned their heads and hurried away. There was no time for Simon to worry about the injustice of it all or how invisible the poor were to so-called respectable people. So few people had been willing to give any of the boys of the park the time of day, let alone stop a man who looked as though he had money and respectability from killing one. The only person who was going to fight to keep Simon alive was himself.

"Get off me," Simon shouted, grabbing Keller's arms and trying with everything he had to pry his hands off his jacket. "I won't let you kill me, like you killed the others."

Keller's eyes went wide. "What do you know about the others?"

If Simon had needed any proof at all that Keller was the one responsible for the deaths of the other boys from the park, that question seemed to settle it. "We all know," he spat at Keller. "All of the boys here know what you've done."

It was a partial lie. They knew there was a killer, but none of them had figured out who that killer was yet. As soon as Simon got away, he would spread Keller's name far and wide.

The burst of determination that came with that thought was squashed a moment later when Keller hit him hard across the face. The blow sent Simon reeling and nearly knocked the sense out of him. He would have fallen if Keller wasn't holding him. Keller hit him a second time, though not as hard, then a third. It was all Simon could do not to lose consciousness at the blows and to stay upright.

"This is all Sullivan's fault," Keller growled as he shifted to close his hands around Simon's neck. "If he had left you to die, I wouldn't have to sully my hands like this." Simon's eyes began to water as he fought for breath that he couldn't draw in. "I should have done more than sack him, I should have killed that bastard too. I'll wring his neck, just like I'm wringing yours, as soon as I find him."

Rage like nothing Simon had ever known poured through him. Keller could hurt him and try to kill him all he wanted, but he would not lift a finger against Todd. Simon kicked Keller's shin as hard as he could. When that shocked Keller enough that he loosened his grip on Simon's neck, Simon kicked again and again.

"Stop it, you whore!" Keller howled in pain, letting go of Simon's neck entirely.

That only encouraged Simon to kick more and harder. He summoned up the courage to throw a punch of his own as well, and when it miraculously landed square on Keller's jaw, causing the man to grunt and stagger to the side, Simon broke away from him and ran.

"Oh, no you don't!" Keller shouted, staggering after him.

Simon's only hope was that he could outrun Keller without drawing the attention of the police. There was no doubt in his mind that if the coppers saw a confrontation between him and Keller, they would take Keller's side. That would be a death sentence. His only hope was to get away from the park as fast as—

He barreled straight into a man walking past on the path before he could finish his thought. The force of the impact nearly knocked the sense out of Simon. The man was younger and fitter than Keller, and he was dressed like an aristocrat.

"Whoa, there," he said in a cheery voice, grasping Simon to keep him steady on his feet. "Watch where you're going, young man."

Simon twisted to see if he could spot Keller, and to get out of the aristocrat's arms. Keller had come out from the shrubs, but as soon as he saw Simon with the aristocrat, he pulled himself to a stop, as if he didn't want to risk bringing the aristocrat into the confrontation.

"Is that man bothering you?" the aristocrat asked, his smile faltering.

Simon nodded quickly, shocked that the aristocrat would be concerned with him being bothered instead of Keller, but too terrified to form words.

"Is that why you're looking for Dandie & Wirth?" the aristocrat asked on.

Simon's eyes went wide. "So you know where they are?"

The aristocrat laughed nervously. Both he and Simon glanced back to Keller—who was brushing his coat off and setting himself to rights and pretending as though nothing were wrong. "I do," the aristocrat went on, "but something tells me we shouldn't talk about it here. Let's go somewhere safe."

Simon nodded, but was helpless to do more than follow after the man as he set off toward Park Lane. Going off with aristocrats had never done him any good in the past, but something about the cheerful young lord that ushered him swiftly through the afternoon wanderers in the park made him feel at ease.

Of course, once they'd left the park and crossed the road, heading up the row of somber, old buildings to a door marked with a small brass plaque that he couldn't read, Simon second-guessed that feeling. He hesitated at the door as the aristocrat pushed it open.

"Don't worry," the young lord said. "I swear to you that

The Chameleon Club is the safest place you could possibly be right now."

Simon stood his ground, tempted to whimper or turn and run. He'd heard stories of what happened to rent-boys who had been lured into clubs, none of them good.

"It's alright," the aristocrat assured him, stepping back to take Simon's hand, then lead him on. "You have to trust me when I say that this is a safe place for men like you and me."

Simon was so shocked by that statement that his eyes popped wide and his resistance crumbled. There was no possible way that the aristocrat actually felt he was the same as Simon in any way, and yet, Simon was certain those were the words he'd said.

As soon as the door shut, sealing Simon inside of the most magnificent lobby he'd ever seen, a strange sort of hush fell over him. The lobby was decorated in a warm shade of marble and hung with chandeliers that shed copious amounts of light through the space. The marble and chandeliers continued into a hallway up a small flight of stairs to one side. Directly across from the door was a wide desk with an older man sitting behind it.

"Ah, Lord Hillsboro," the older man said. "What have you got there?"

"This is the young man who has been asking after Dandie & Wirth all day," the aristocrat, Lord Hillsboro, said, gesturing for Simon to approach the desk with him. "And I have the feeling I might have just rescued him from a dangerous situation on top of that."

"How fortunate, though he looks a little worse for wear," the older man said, smiling at Simon. Smiling at him *kindly*, not as though he were a pickpocket or a dirty beggar there to cause trouble and leave smudge marks on the marble. It was enough to have Simon wondering if the soot that had covered him after cleaning out fireplaces hid the marks from the blows Keller had landed on him. It would explain why the men didn't realize he'd been beaten. "Perhaps we can all finally solve the mystery of why the lad is after David and Lionel's help."

Simon blinked at the man, no idea what his words meant.

"Yes, young man," Lord Hillsboro said, his smile fully back in place now that they were in the confines of the club. "We've been speculating all day. What need does a boy from the park have for the services of a solicitor?"

Simon gulped and glanced between the two men. "I...that is...my friend went to see them. Dr. Sullivan. A man named Mercer gave him a card for Dandie & Wirth to help find him a position in a hospital as a surgeon. Only, I have to find him before he goes back to his family's house. Keller was there, and he's the one who killed the other boys and who tried to kill me. But he's not at Todd's family's house now, he's in the park. Just now. And he tried to kill me again."

Simon hadn't intended to blurt out the whole story like that, but as soon as he did, Lord Hillsboro and the man behind the desk went serious.

"Is that what happened to you out there?" Lord Hillsboro asked, taking a closer look at Simon.

Simon nodded, his eyes stinging with tears. He hated that he was falling apart like a child in front of these men, but he was hurt, exhausted, and he longed for Todd so desperately that it made his physical injuries pale in comparison.

"Dammit, you're injured," Lord Hillsboro said, seeming to notice at last. "I'm so sorry I didn't notice. Let's get you cleaned up, then we'll see if we can't send someone to David and Lionel to find out what happened to your friend."

Simon was too overcome with emotion and delayed panic after his encounter with Keller to protest or fight as Lord Hillsboro took his arm and led him up the short flight of stairs and along the hall.

"What is your name?" Lord Hillsboro asked, then added, "I'm sorry, I should have asked before. It's just that when word reached the club that a waif of some sort was looking for David and Lionel, I'm afraid we all took it far less seriously than we should have."

"Not David and Lionel," Simon mumbled as Lord Hillsboro escorted him past several small, beautiful parlors, "Dandie & Wirth."

"Yes, it's David Wirth and his assistant, Lionel Mercer. The office is called Dandie & Wirth because David started it years ago with his partner, John Dandie. They split, though, and John has moved on to Manchester, but David has Lionel now, and—and I don't know why I'm bothering you with these details." Lord Hillsboro laughed.

Simon hardly noticed. Lord Hillsboro turned a corner, leading Simon into a massive room that took his breath away. It was all gilded and gorgeous, with beautiful paintings on the wall, sumptuous carpets on the floor, tall windows at the far end, and, best of all, a long table off to one side that was piled high with food of every description. In the short glance that he got, Simon could see cold meats and cheeses, pies and pastries, tea and some sort of punch in a giant, silver bowl, and a platter of roasted vegetables. His mouth instantly began to water, and his stomach growled.

"We'll feed you up as soon as we get you scrubbed and whatever wounds you have seen to," Lord Hillsboro promised. "Though I'm not sure if anyone present today has the slightest bit of medical training."

He glanced across the room as the two of them walked. In addition to the table of food, dozens of round tables were set up throughout the room, as if someone was hosting a perpetual banquet. A few men sat around the tables, but not nearly as many as there was space provided for. A distracted man with light hair sat at one table with pages and pages of paper in front of him, scribbling away as he wrote something. A gentleman who looked African sat at another table with a garishly-dressed man who Simon could have sworn was the famous actor, Everett Jewel. He'd seen the man's likeness on posters outside of theaters, but he'd never dreamed he'd see the man in person. Jewell and the African man were taking turns singing something and laughing about it.

But it was another man who snagged Simon's attention, causing him to gasp out loud. Mr. Albright, the reporter, sat at one of the tables with a large, gruff-looking police officer, eating what looked like a sandwich of some sort and chatting.

"There's a lavatory right over here," Lord Hillsboro explained as he and Simon neared a door on the far side of the room. "We can get you clean in there at the very least, then find someone to tend to what I can now see are bruises or abrasions on your face and neck. Does that sound—"

"Mr. Albright!" Simon called out, breaking away from Lord Hillsboro as politely as he could and waving to the reporter.

Mr. Albright stopped in the middle of whatever he was saying and glanced across the room at Simon. As soon as he recognized Simon, his eyes went wide. "Simon, is it?" Mr. Albright called back as Simon made his way across the room, dodging around tables and ducking past some of the gentlemen who were milling around. "What has happened to you, young man?" Albright asked when Simon reached him.

"I know who the killer is," Simon panted, out of breath from his sojourn across the room. "It's a man named Keller. He's still in Hyde Park, and he just tried to kill me again."

Nine

It was late by the time Todd and Mercer headed back to Mercer and his partner's office. Todd was as restless and out of sorts as he'd ever been. He felt like a vagabond carrying all of his belongings in a suitcase with him. The situations they'd encountered at the hospital, the way Keller had deliberately blocked him from finding employment as a surgeon, had every last one of Todd's nerves standing on end. Mercer attempted to distract him by asking about possible medical treatments for a certain condition that, it didn't take Todd long to figure out, Mercer himself might be suffering from.

"I will gladly treat you using whatever methods you wish to try," he told Mercer as they stepped into the building housing Mercer and his partner's office as the shadows grew long and the light dimmed, "even experimental ones. But you do understand there is no cure for that particular malady, and the prognosis is not good."

Mercer was uncharacteristically quiet and forlorn as they stepped into the office itself. "Too many things in this world have a prognosis that is not good," he said. The troubled expression he wore had Todd wondering what sort of challenges the beautiful, charismatic, surprisingly intimidating man might have.

But there were other things much closer to Todd's heart that needed his attention first. "I need to go," he told Mercer, not removing his hat and coat when Mercer removed his. "I need to find my friend, Simon. He is deeply vulnerable, and I fear that he could be in danger if I don't find him."

"Are you afraid he'll return to his former profession?" Mercer asked, as casual as could be, as he crossed to the desk and picked up a small note resting there.

Heat and embarrassment flooded Todd's cheeks. He hadn't explicitly said what Simon was—or rather, what he had been—but he must have given Mercer enough of an idea through talking about him that day for the man to guess.

"I do not think he would go back to that, no," he said, surprised at how deeply he believed it. Simon was his now, and though they hadn't spoken about it directly, Todd was certain they both knew it beyond a shadow of a doubt. "He is young and vulnerable, though," he went on. "He might not go looking for trouble, but trouble could come for him."

Todd wasn't certain whether Mercer heard a word he said. Mercer's expression fell into a frown as he read the note from his desk.

"We have to go to The Chameleon Club at once," he said, striding back to the rack by the door to don his coat and hat again.

Todd winced slightly, fighting down a wave of irritation over the way it appeared that Mercer had just ignored everything he'd said about needing to find the love of his life before Simon fell into danger. "I will not keep you," he said, heading right back out to the street with Mercer, "but I need to search for Simon."

"David's note said that you need to come as well," Mercer

said, as though that was something that couldn't be argued with.

Todd frowned, but followed Mercer to the end of the street, where he reached out a hand to hail a cab. "I do appreciate that, but Simon is my priority." He paused. "Unless your friend mentioned something about Simon in his note."

"Not as such," Mercer said, smiling a bit when a carriage pulled around toward them.

"Then I must decline his invitation," Todd said, not knowing how else he could make his intentions clear.

Mercer turned to him as the cabbie hopped down to hold the carriage door open for them. "Do you know where your friend Simon might've gone?" he asked.

Todd's mouth dropped open, but he didn't have a ready answer. He rubbed the back of his neck, thought about it for a moment, then said, "The only place I can think of is Hyde Park, since he has friends there."

Mercer nodded as though that answer were obvious. "The Chameleon Club is on Park Lane, as I believe I've mentioned. One way or another, we're going to the same place."

It was an argument Todd couldn't refute. He had no choice but to climb into the carriage with Mercer, feeling more than a little sheepish as he did.

"I will find a way to repay you for your help today," he said as the carriage lurched into motion, hopefully taking him closer to Simon. "For the omnibus fare, for this cab, for lunch. I have no money at all to my name right now, but I will find a way to repay you."

Mercer smiled a lovely and enigmatic smile as he settled on the seat across from Todd. "As it happens, I already have an idea of how you might do that. But first things first. We must join David at the club to see what he wants and we must find your man."

It was a testament of how strange and revelatory the day

was that Todd barely flinched at Mercer's intimation that Simon was his lover. It was true, but Todd was far from used to having such things spoken of openly.

There wasn't much to say on the ride to Park Lane. Todd was exhausted from what amounted to two days of constant, restless motion. He could have done with a rest. Once he found Simon, the two of them would find a way—though God only knew how—to simply rest for as long as it took the two of them to feel whole again.

There was a great deal of traffic approaching Park Lane, so rather than wait impatiently, Todd and Mercer departed the cab closer to Hyde Park Corner than the mysterious location of The Chameleon Club.

"It's a little more than halfway up the street this way," Mercer said, nodding at the crowded path.

"And Hyde Park is right over there," Todd said, peeling away from Mercer and taking advantage of a sudden gap in traffic to dash across the street.

"Sullivan, where are you going?" Mercer called after him, sounding more than a little annoyed.

Todd was highly aware that attempting to leave Mercer behind was horrifically rude, but if he had to be rude to keep his priorities in line, then so be it. He dodged around a few gentlemen in some sort of argument near the entrance to the park, then narrowly avoided tripping over a young man selling the evening edition of some newspaper.

Mercer caught up to him as he started along one of the many lanes cutting through the park. "If you think this is the best way to find your friend, I suppose I can indulge you," he said with a sigh. "But if David said that we should both come to the club, we should both have gone to the club."

Todd sent Mercer a sideways look as he attempted to keep his temper in check. "We can go to your club once we find Simon," he said. "I would be far too agitated and worried for my friend to enjoy whatever amenities your club has to offer if I went there without reuniting with my friend."

"I suppose I understand," Mercer sighed again.

Evening had well and truly fallen by the time they were near the section of the park where Todd had treated the rent-boys the day before. It wasn't quite full dark yet, and the lamps placed here and there along the paths shed a bit of light, but it was dim enough to lend a somewhat menacing air to the otherwise cheerful park. In the shadows, Todd could already see the less savory side of London life unfolding. He had no doubt that everything from prostitution to smuggling was going on around him. The Metropolitan Police did their best to curb illegal activities in London's parks, but they were outnumbered by the sheer volume of mischief around them.

That thought was rolling around Todd's mind when he caught a hint of movement out of the corner of his eye that gave him pause. He threw out a hand to stop Mercer in his tracks, then squinted into the dark to make certain what he thought he was seeing was actually what he saw.

Near the corner of one of the clusters of shrubs, a man in a greatcoat and top hat had just dragged a young man out of the shrub and was shaking him. Not just any man, though —Keller.

"Where is he?" Todd was just able to make out Keller's vicious growl. "Where is the bastard?"

The sight of the man who had caused him so much injury had Todd's temper flaring in no time. "Keller!" he called out, veering off the path and marching toward him. He would give the blackguard a piece of his mind if it was the last thing he ever did. "Keller, you snake, come over here and face me. I know what you did to me."

Keller jerked straight and pushed the young man he'd been accosting aside so fast that the lad fell. Todd briefly recognized him as Oliver, one of Simon's friends, but he didn't have time to acknowledge the man. Keller's eyes went wide in the dim light for a moment before narrowing, "You don't know anything," he growled.

Todd barely registered how incongruous the comment was. He marched closer to Keller and said, "You have somehow managed to spread poison at every hospital in London, and now none of them will give me a position. How dare you attempt to ruin my life in such an underhanded way?"

Instead of arguing or defending himself, Keller laughed. "Yes," he said. "My greatest crime is squashing the career of a third-rate surgeon from a disgraced family of quacks."

The hair stood up on the back of Todd's neck at the statement. It didn't fit at all with the argument he thought they were having. "I demand you reverse whatever devilry you've put into place and clear my name with—"

"Dr. Sullivan!" Oliver gasped suddenly from the shadows at the edge of the shrubs, as if he'd just recognized who Todd was. "Dr. Sullivan, he's a murderer," Oliver rushed on, pointing at Keller. "He's the one what's been doing in the boys."

Todd's heart seemed to stop in his chest for a moment, and he snapped his gaze back to Keller. Keller's face had drained of color, making him look downright spectral in the dim light. His look wasn't one of indignation at being accused of something ridiculous, it was the horror of being found out for what he was.

In a flash, everything made sense. Todd had found Simon next to the hospital where Keller was at work. When he'd brought Simon in for treatment, Keller had tried to get rid of him, going so far as sacking Todd. He hadn't done it because of any moral compunction about treating a whore, he'd done it because if Simon had recovered, he could identify Keller as the man who had nearly killed him. The other boys in the park must have had some inkling of who was committing the murders, but they wouldn't have had a name to put to the face. Because of his connection to Todd and Todd's connection to Keller, Simon would. Simon was in more danger than Todd had dreamed possible.

"You tried to kill him," Todd gasped. "You would have killed him if I hadn't saved him. Oliver is right. You are a murderer."

"You can't prove anything," Keller growled. But he must have known that Todd, with Simon's help, could indeed prove everything.

Keller turned and ran. He had enough of a jump on him that even when Todd—and Mercer behind him—leapt into pursuit, he stayed a few steps ahead. The park was far emptier after dark than it had been during the day, but that only meant that Keller was able to run faster and harder, without random pedestrians getting in his way.

"Stop!" Todd shouted, even though he knew Keller wouldn't. "You won't get away with this. You're a murderer, and you will pay!"

Even though the park was less crowded, it wasn't entirely empty. Todd and Mercer had to dodge a few men who shuffled along the paths, looking as though they were up to no good, and a few women who looked as though they were there on business. Keller was surprisingly fit, but so was Todd, and Mercer had far more stamina than Todd would have guessed from his delicate appearance and fine clothes. That didn't help to end the chase, though. In fact, Keller seemed to be on the verge of getting away.

The shrill cry of a policeman's whistle as they neared Cumberland Gate startled Todd nearly to the point of tripping over his feet. Fortunately, it startled Keller as well. Keller jerked to one side, stumbling. A moment later, the policeman who had blown the whistle leapt toward him. Keller let out a wordless cry and tried to run, but the policeman was built like a prize-fighter and quick to boot. He tackled Keller, throwing them both to the grass by the side of the path.

"That was a little dramatic, don't you think, Patrick?" Mercer called out, breathless but sounding amused by the whole thing, as he and Todd jogged to a stop by the side of the path where the officer had Keller.

"Don't struggle," the officer warned Keller in a deep, rumbling voice. "You're under arrest for the murders of half a dozen young men."

"This is preposterous," Keller shouted, thrashing. "Don't you know who I am? You can prove nothing. I'll have your hide for this."

"Actually, we can prove quite a bit." Todd was surprised enough to flinch as Albright jogged over to join the scene, as if he'd been part of the chase as well. "I've been compiling information about this story for weeks now," he went on. "And finally, I have the last bit of information I need to complete the story—the name of the killer."

"This is unacceptable," Keller growled, continuing to thrash and struggle, even though the police officer had him thoroughly secured. "You can prove nothing."

"We have a witness who is willing to testify that you attempted to murder him on the night of June third, just outside of St. Andrew's Hospital," the officer said.

Todd sucked in a breath, his throat closing up and his heart hammering. "Simon," he said, glancing from the officer to Albright. "Where is Simon? Is he safe? Is he in danger? What has happened to him?"

"Your young man is perfectly safe," Albright told him, coming over to clap a hand on Todd's shoulder. Again, the openness that Albright expressed in implying a relationship between him and Simon sent a chill down Todd's back. Albright must have been a part of this brotherhood that Mercer had told him about earlier.

"Where is he?" Todd asked, keeping his voice down all the same. The others might have no qualms about speaking openly about such things, but Todd had yet to be convinced the officer pinning Keller wouldn't turn around and arrest them all for indecency.

Then again, Mercer had addressed the man by his first name. That seemed to hint that the officer was a member of the Brotherhood as well.

"Simon is safe at the club, where he's been since this morning," Albright reassured him with a smile. "He had a run-in with Keller earlier today, but Hillsboro found him before greater harm could come to him. Simon has been very brave in the information he has shared with us today. The Brotherhood has been aware of the murders of young men taking place, but up until today, we haven't had enough information to give to the police so that they could make an arrest. Thanks to your young man, now we do."

"No," Keller wailed in the grass. "No, I won't accept it. You dare to take some dirty whore's word over mine?"

The officer punched the side of Keller's face hard enough to stun Keller into silence. "Oops," he mumbled. "I slipped."

Mercer barked a laugh.

The mood seemed to have lightened considerably for everyone except Todd.

"Take me to Simon," he said, still in a state of near panic. "I have to see that he's safe."

"Of course," Albright said. "Right this way."

Ten

Simon paced restlessly near the table where his new friends—if he was allowed to consider the famous African composer, Samuel Percy, and the even more famous actor, Everett Jewell, and a solicitor, Mr. David Wirth, as his friends—were seated. They were laughing at him, Simon was certain, but he couldn't bring himself to care. He'd been laughed at for much worse than worrying himself to shreds over his lover. How could he not worry, though? Todd was out there, somewhere in London, and Keller was too. If Keller found Todd, it could be a disaster.

"You've nothing to worry about, lad," Mr. Percy told Simon in his deep, booming voice. "Albright has set all the right wheels in motion to catch Keller."

"And that fetching officer will certainly bring him to justice," Jewell added, a twinkle in his eye that befitted his name.

"I am very grateful to them," Simon said. But he wouldn't be able to rest easy until he was back in Todd's arms.

"Come and have some supper at least," Mr. Wirth told him. "The kitchen has outdone itself tonight with this lamb."

The lamb was nearly enough to tempt Simon to give up his pacing. He glanced around the dining room—which was now three times as crowded with men of every description. At one glance, he could see noblemen and tradesmen, tough, burly men and slender dandies, men of different nationalities, and a few who, by all appearances, were women, complete with gowns and cosmetics. In the hours since Simon had been brought to The Chameleon Club that morning and introduced to the Brotherhood, a whole new world of safety and camaraderie had embraced him.

It was more than just the variety of the men who were members of the club. Simon had been in a state that morning, and after Albright had left to set things in motion to go after Keller, Lord Hillsboro had taken Simon to one of the private chambers upstairs and had the most sumptuous bath Simon had ever taken drawn for him.

Other members of the Brotherhood had arrived at the door with clean clothing, new shoes, and even the offer of a haircut for Simon. Then Mr. Wirth—Simon was so relieved to solve the mystery of Dandie & Wirth that he nearly cried when the man introduced himself—came and asked questions about the night he was almost killed. He'd sworn that Keller would be brought to justice and that Todd would be safe.

They had fed him, made certain he was scrubbed and that the bruises and cuts Keller had left on his face were treated—though not as thoroughly as Todd would be able to treat them—and had spent the afternoon asking about his life. That had led to more questions about the boys in the park—who they were all aware of and did their best to help as much as they could—and about Keller.

"He's clearly too worried about his sweetheart to eat anything," Jewell commented to Mr. Percy as Simon continued to pace and dwell in his thoughts. "I'd be just as twisted up with anxiety if I had a lover who was in danger."

"Don't you have at least a dozen lovers?" Percy teased him.

"I do not," Jewell said with pretend offense. "Why settle for one lover, or a dozen, when I can have my pick at the stage door each night after every performance?"

Mr. Percy roared with laughter and Mr. Wirth shook his head, but the reactions, and Mr. Jewell's statement, only made Simon uneasy. He wasn't sure if Jewell was joking, but either way, Simon knew now that he would rather have just Todd as his one and only lover for the rest of his life instead of going with whatever gentleman crooked his finger and ordered him to his knees every night.

That thought came right as there was a small commotion near the doorway. Simon turned with anxious curiosity, but his heart burst with joy a moment later when he saw that the commotion was Mr. Albright returning, and Todd was with him.

With a wordless cry of relief, Simon broke away from the table and dashed across the room to Todd. He was vaguely aware of all eyes in the room fixing on them, but he didn't care. Todd spotted him and burst into the same sort of relieved shout, moving away from Mr. Albright and the other man with him. He opened his arms as Simon reached him and grunted at the impact of their bodies slamming together in an embrace. That grunt was followed by laughter that Simon shared.

"You're safe," Simon gasped, grasping the sides of his angel's face and beaming up at him. "I was so worried Keller would find you, after I saw him at your family's house, and that he would do something to harm you."

"And I was terrified that he had found and hurt you," Todd replied. His joy fell into concern a moment later when he saw the state of Simon's face. He touched the bruises there and turned Simon's head this way and that to assess the damage. "He did find you, didn't he?"

Simon nodded, tears stinging his eyes. They were happy tears, though. He didn't care about bruises and cuts. Not when he was safe in Todd's arms.

"You'll be pleased to know, young Simon, that Dr. Keller was just arrested in Hyde Park," Albright said.

Simon gasped and dragged his gaze away from Todd to stare at Mr. Albright. "He was?"

"Yes," the other man with Todd and Mr. Albright said, coming forward. When Mr. Wirth walked over to stand next to the man, Simon assumed he had to be Mr. Mercer. "Patrick has carted him off to Scotland Yard, or wherever nefarious murderers are housed before being strung up by their neck."

Simon lifted a hand to his bruised neck, feeling a horrible chill at Mr. Mercer's statement. He was glad Keller would be brought to justice, but the whole thing still frightened him.

Todd seemed to sense as much and pulled Simon into his arms. "He can't hurt you now," his angel promised. "No one can hurt you. I won't let them."

Simon let out a breath and sagged against Todd. It was the most wonderful feeling in the world to be promised safety and comfort by the man he adored more than anything. It also astounded him that the other men around them glanced on in approval, grinning and looking pleased. Mr. Wirth sent a longing look to Mr. Mercer, but Simon wasn't certain if Mr. Mercer noticed or if he returned the man's affection.

When the silence surrounding the group began to grow awkward, Todd inched back from Simon a bit, looked at the others, and said, "I will find a way to repay you all. I don't know how, but I will. For now, at least, I think it would be best if Simon and I left so that we might figure out how we will put a roof over our head tonight."

"As to that," Mr. Wirth said, a mischievous smile on his face, "I've talked to the others, and we've come up with an idea."

"The others?" Todd asked. Simon felt him tense.

"The members of the Brotherhood who are currently taking a turn at administrating our business, I presume," Mercer said.

"Indeed," Wirth nodded. "It has occurred to us as we saw to your Simon's needs today that the Brotherhood could use a trained man of medicine among its ranks. One who might be able to serve the unique needs of our membership without question or judgement."

Todd blinked at Wirth. "You…you wish to hire me?"

"I was going to suggest as much myself at the first opportunity," Mercer said.

"The position would come with a stipend, of course," Wirth went on. "And rooms right here, at The Chameleon Club."

Simon's heart quivered with joy in his chest. The very idea that he might be able to stay at the opulent club, that he could make it his home, was beyond his wildest imaginations.

A moment later, however, his spirits dropped. There was no guarantee that Todd would want to keep him, particularly if he were to make a place such as The Chameleon Club his new home.

"I'm not sure what to say," Todd replied to Mr. Wirth, clearly stunned. "This is an offer I never could have expected and am not prepared for."

"It is an offer that is being made nonetheless," Mr. Albright said, as though he had been a part of whatever conversations Mr. Wirth had had about it that afternoon instead of spending his time chasing after Keller. He glanced to Simon with a grin and said, "I am certain young Simon would be happy to stay here."

All eyes were suddenly on Simon, which caused him to shrink in on himself. "That is…if…if you still want me," he said to Todd, his voice diminishing with each statement until it was a bare whisper.

Todd's eyes shone with love and tenderness. He caressed the sides of Simon's face and smiled at him in a way that had Simon's soul singing. "My darling, I want you more than I have ever wanted anything. I could not bear to be parted from you. Not now and not ever." He turned to Mr. Wirth. "I can only accept your kind offer if Simon is allowed to stay with me. I could train him as my assistant, if that helps."

"Your assistant?" Simon gasped. When Todd looked back at him, he asked, "You mean, you would teach me how to heal people and treat the sick?"

"I would," Todd said, beaming. "And I would need your help convincing the boys in the park to let me treat them, I think." He blinked, then turned to the others. "Would you consent to allow me to give medical care to those in need, such as the boys in the park, in addition to whatever duties you would have me perform for the men of this club?"

"Of course," Mercer said with a bright smile. "I believe the members of the Brotherhood would encourage it."

Todd smiled from ear to ear. "Then I accept your offer of a position," he said, looking as though he hardly believed his luck. He reached for Simon's hand and squeezed it. "We both accept it."

"You do realize," Mr. Albright interrupted the happy moment, holding up a hand, "that as soon as I publish my article detailing the capture of Keller and the life of the unfortunate young men in Hyde Park—a story in which I fully intend to highlight your nobility in treating them for their maladies—you could likely accept any position at any hospital in London or beyond."

Todd's brow flew up. A moment later, he glanced to Simon, and his expression evened out to affection and gratitude. "I think I see now that my calling is not to treat those who have the liberty of seeking out the finest medical care at a hospital or Harley Street practice, but rather those who, for various reasons, have not been privileged enough to receive that sort of treatment."

"Then I am certain that all of the members of the Brotherhood will agree we've made the right decision in hiring you as our very own," Mr. Wirth said. "And now, I can imagine that it has been a trying day for you, and as I mentioned to your Simon earlier, the kitchen has outdone themselves with the roast lamb, and I would be willing to wager that you could use a heaping plate of it to fill your stomach."

"I most certainly could," Todd said, nearly sagging with gratitude.

Simon suddenly had an appetite as well, and once the two of them were seated side by side at one of the tables, the members of the club practically fell all over themselves bringing food and drink, and pudding after all that was consumed. When the meal was done, another member of the club escorted them upstairs to one of the guest rooms that was currently made up. They were promised a grander suite in a few days' time, once preparations for their permanent residence could be made, but for the time being, the guest room was more than enough.

"This is the grandest place I've ever slept in," Simon said as he stood in the center of the room, turning a slow circle and gawping at everything from the embossed wallpaper to the cheerful fireplace to the lavish carpet that covered the floor. He finished his circle by staring at the large, richly-appointed bed and blushed.

"These men are uncommonly kind," Todd said from the other side of a doorway leading into perhaps the most magnificent feature of the room—a fully-plumbed washroom. Todd had taken a bath as soon as they'd come up from supper, but since Simon had taken one that afternoon, he'd amused himself by exploring the room instead. "They have no reason to be kind to us," Todd went on as he stepped out of the washroom, dressed only in a robe.

"I think they believe, as I do now, that we all have to be kind to each other," Simon said, only half thinking about the words coming from him. He was too enamored of the sight of Todd fresh from his bath, his hair still damp and his skin pink and warm-looking.

"You're right," Todd said, his smile turning amorous as he crossed the room to Simon. "There are enough forces working against men like us already. We have to take care of each other. That is what I like most about this brotherhood and why I am so pleased to accept a position as their personal physician. There is only one thing that makes me happier than knowing an organization such as this exists."

"And what is that?" Simon asked, his face heating like a furnace, guessing the answer. He sent Todd a bashful but passionate look, head tilted down slightly.

As he expected, Todd took him into his arms and held him intimately close. Simon was still dressed, but only in his shirt and trousers, and the embrace felt wonderful. Even more wonderful was the way Todd slanted his mouth over his in a tender kiss before answering, "You. You make me so happy, Simon."

"I love you," Simon blurted before he could think better of it. It was such a rash and clumsy thing to say.

But Todd's smile grew, and he murmured back, "And I love you, my darling."

Those words and the kiss that followed them sent joy like Simon had never known racing through him. He slipped his arms around Todd's back and held him as they devoured each other. Todd still didn't know much about proper kissing, but Simon was more than willing to teach him. He would teach Todd everything.

With that in mind, he tugged at the sash of Todd's robe and scrambled to push it off his shoulders. Then he tugged at the hem of his own shirt, tearing it off over his head. Todd laughed affectionately as Simon fumbled through the fastenings of his trousers and said, "I love your eagerness and your enthusiasm."

"I just want to be with you," Simon panted as he shoved at his trousers and drawers, kicking them off unceremoniously, then plastering himself against Todd once more. "I want to be with you fully. And I want to be with you forever."

"That's what I want too," Todd answered breathlessly. The sudden tension in his body combined with the uncertainty that pinched his face hinted to Simon that his angel was worried he might be a disappointment.

"I'll tell you what you need to do," Simon promised him, kissing Todd's parted lips quickly, then shifting to rain kisses across his shoulders. "I'll tell you and I'll show you. Don't be afraid. I love you, and I just want you to love me."

"I do," Todd said, sucking in a breath as Simon kissed his way down to one of his nipples. "I will."

Simon indulged in tasting Todd's nipple for a moment, but he was impatient for more. He straightened and took Todd's hand, leading him over to the bed. He pulled back the covers to reveal crisp, white sheets spread over the softest mattress Simon had ever known. He climbed onto the bed, reaching for a jar that he'd found conveniently tucked into the drawer on the bedside table when he'd explored the room earlier.

"What is that?" Todd asked, nervousness still in his voice as he joined Simon on the bed.

"It's the slippery stuff," Simon explained. "To make things easier."

Todd flushed a darker shade of pink. "Yes, of course," he said, taking the jar and removing the top. "I should have known." He dabbed a finger into the clear substance, then rubbed his two fingers together.

"It's alright if you didn't know," Simon said, relaxing onto his back with his head against the numerous, plush pillows.

Todd continued to look uncertain. "So I just…er…spread it on myself, or you?"

In spite of his vow to be patient and understanding, Simon laughed. "Kiss me first," he said, holding out his arms for his angel.

Todd grinned and set the open jar aside. "I can do that," he said.

He positioned himself between Simon's open legs, then lowered himself with a groan of pleasure until their bodies were flush against each other. Simon lifted his legs to hook over Todd's hips and wrapped his arms around Todd's lean sides and muscular back. He wished he had enough fancy words to tell Todd how good it felt to have his weight atop him and their bodies sliding together, but all he had were kisses and the language of his body. He pulled Todd's head closer and brought their mouths together with more passion than he'd ever felt for a man. The men who had hired him in the past rarely wanted to kiss, so it felt different and special for their lips and tongues to tease and taste each other than it ever had with Simon before.

"This is so lovely," Simon sighed at length, threading his

fingers through Todd's hair and reveling in how safe it felt to be sexual with another man, for a change.

"Yes, it is," Todd purred in return. "I almost feel like I know what I'm doing."

Simon giggled. "You're doing wonderfully."

Encouraged by that, Todd imitated what Simon had done earlier and kissed his way down Simon's neck to his shoulder, then across to the other shoulder, then down to lick one of Simon's nipples. He moaned as though he were the one being treated instead of the other way around. Better still, Simon felt the hot, thick spear of Todd's cock pressing against his thigh. His own cock pulsed with arousal, anticipating how good it would feel when the two of them were joined at last.

Todd drew in a sudden breath, lifting away from Simon for a moment with a passion-hazy look. "I don't think I'm going to last," he gasped. "I want to. God knows I want to. But it's all too new. It's too much. I need—"

Simon pressed a finger to his lips and whispered, "Shh. It's alright. We have more than enough time to touch and kiss and pet each other until we're both dizzy. Let me show you what we both want right now."

Todd gazed down at him with a look filled with more love and trust than Simon had ever known and nodded. It was enough to bring Simon close to tears. Just over a fortnight ago, he had nearly died at the hands of the Devil. Now he was in the arms of an angel who would never let him go.

He reached for the jar, and scooped a generous amount of its contents onto his fingers. Then he reached between him and Todd, slicking Todd's cock and making him groan and shudder as he did. With a few nudges, he guided Todd to lift up a bit, which not only gave Simon more room to play with his cock, it enabled him to draw his own legs up and lift his hips to open himself fully to his angel. He used what was left in his fingers to prepare his hole, shamelessly penetrating himself with one, then two fingers while Todd watched. A part of him would have liked to do far more salacious things to himself while Todd watched, but he could see the need in Todd's eyes and knew he needed to help his lover fulfill that need.

Using looks and movements only, he positioned himself and Todd so that the head of Todd's cock pressed against his hole, then he nodded.

Todd leaned into him, breeching him just slightly, then asked in a tremulous voice, "Are you certain?"

"Yes," Simon gasped, gripping Todd's sides and pushing into him. "Oh, yes."

Todd let out a shaky breath, then moved into him. They both gasped and vocalized their pleasure and wonder, but Simon wanted more. He made a plaintive sound, arching against Todd to draw him deeper. Whether through his own efforts or because instinct took over in Todd, Todd surged into him, slowly driving deep until their bodies were flush against each other.

"Yes, oh, yes, my angel," Simon cried out, gripping Todd harder and urging him to move.

Todd made a sound of triumph and pulled back enough so that he could plunge in again. Then again and again, picking up speed with every thrust. Everything about it was perfect and wonderful. Todd grabbed Simon's hips, holding him steady while his thrust grew in confidence and power. It was everything Simon had ever wanted. He could sense that, as he'd predicted, Todd wouldn't last long, so he grasped his own cock with the hand that was still slick with lubricant and pumped as Todd impaled him.

Todd let out a gasp and a moan moments later, jerking a few more times. That was all Simon needed to let himself go and spill all over his belly and chest. Todd groaned again as

Simon's body contracted with orgasm, as if he hadn't expected that sensation at all. There were so many sensations and feelings that the two of them had yet to explore, but for now, Simon was satisfied and happier than he'd ever been.

"I love you so dearly," he purred as Todd pulled out of him and the two of them settled on their sides in a tangle of overheated arms and legs.

"And I love you," Todd said in return, smiling and brushing a hand along the side of Simon's face. "And I swear to you, no one will ever part the two of us for the rest of our lives."

Author's Note: It's hard to believe in our modern world of nationalized healthcare for some and complicated bureaucracy and insurance for others, but in the late-Victorian Era in England, the idea of going to school to study medicine was a brand-new thing. For centuries, physicians and medical men were trained through apprenticeship, or they had no training at all. There were no requirements for calling oneself a doctor. That was why you ended up with physicians doing more harm than good. History is riddled with stories of quack doctors killing or permanently maiming their patients through the use of made-up remedies or sheer incompetence. The idea that Todd's father was run out of medicine for gross negligence was a common thing. The fact that Todd had studied at a prestigious institution and still had trouble finding a job wasn't as uncommon as you might think either. The 1880s were a strange sort of transition time in the medical field, and a lot of the old guard still clung to the way things had been when they were young.

Also, while a lot of Historical Romance readers—or modern vacationers—like to think of Hyde Park as the scene of ladies and gentlemen strolling out and meeting up for quite proper social events, in actuality, Hyde Park—and all of the other parks in London—was a notorious location of illicit activities for hundreds of years. It was particularly known for prostitution, especially after dark. So it isn't a stretch at all to imagine Simon, Robbie, Oliver, and their friends making the park their home and place of business.

I hope you have enjoyed *Just a Little Prelude*! This prequel novella has introduced not only the Brotherhood and The Chameleon Club, but several of the characters who take center stage in the other books of my Victorian M/M Romance series, *The Brotherhood*. If you keep reading, you'll get to know a lot more about Maxwell Hillsboro, Officer Patrick Wrexham, Everett Jewell, Samuel Percy, and, of course, Lionel Mercer and David Wirth. Get started on the adventures of *The Brotherhood* today with *Just a Little Wickedness*!

You can also reconnect with Marcus Albright as he makes his own connections with another character from *The Brotherhood* series, Jasper Werther! Their story is the first book in a Gilded Age series set in New York City in the 1890s, *The Slippery Slope*. Be sure to look for Marcus and Jasper's story, *A Touch of Romance*.

If you enjoyed this book and would like to hear more from me, please sign up for my newsletter! When you sign up, you'll get a free, full-length novella, *A Passionate Deception*. Victorian identity theft has never been so exciting in this story of hope, tricks, and starting over. Part of my West Meets East series, *A Passionate Deception* can be read as a stand-alone. It is an M/F Romance, but it introduces a few key characters in my M/M books. Pick up your free copy today by signing up to receive my newsletter (which I only send out when I have a new release)!

Sign up here: http://eepurl.com/cbaVMH

Are you on social media? I am! Come and join the fun on Facebook: http://www.facebook.com/merryfarmerreaders

I'm also a huge fan of Instagram and post lots of original content there: https://www.instagram.com/merryfarmer/

About the Author

I hope you have enjoyed *Just a Little Prelude*. If you'd like to be the first to learn about when new books in the series come out and more, please sign up for my newsletter here: http://eepurl.com/cbaVMH And remember, Read it, Review it, Share it! For a complete list of works by Merry Farmer with links, please visit http://wp.me/P5ttjb-14F.

USA Today Bestselling author Merry Farmer is an award-winning novelist who lives in suburban Philadelphia with her cats, Justine and Peter. She has been writing since she was ten years old and realized one day that she didn't have to wait for the teacher to assign a creative writing project to write something. It was the best day of her life. She then went on to earn not one but two degrees in History so that she would always have something to write about. Her books have reached the Top 100 at Amazon, iBooks, and Barnes & Noble, and have been named finalists in the prestigious RONE and Rom Com Reader's Crown awards.

Acknowledgments

I owe a huge debt of gratitude to my awesome beta-readers, Caroline Lee and Jolene Stewart, for their suggestions and advice. And double thanks to Julie Tague, for being a truly excellent editor and to Cindy Jackson for being an awesome assistant!

Click here for a complete list of other works by Merry Farmer.

Printed in Great Britain
by Amazon